Pelican Books

Inflation
A Guide to the Crisis in Economic

James Trevithick is a Fellow of King's College,
Cambridge and University Lecturer in Economics.
He is the co-author (with C. Mulvey) of *The Economics
of Inflation* (1975) and the author of several papers on
both the theoretical and empirical aspects of inflation.
In this respect he has been particularly concerned with
adapting Keynes's methods of analysis to cope with
the problem of inflation. He is currently engaged
in an examination of the evolution of Keynes's views
on monetary policy after the *General Theory*.

Inflation

A Guide to the Crisis in Economics

J. A. Trevithick

Second Edition

Penguin Books

Penguin Books Ltd, Harmondsworth, Middlesex, England
Viking Penguin Inc., 40 West 23rd Street, New York, New York 10010, U.S.A.
Penguin Books Australia Ltd, Ringwood, Victoria, Australia
Penguin Books Canada Ltd, 2801 John Street, Markham, Ontario, Canada L3R 1B4
Penguin Books (N.Z.) Ltd, 182–190 Wairau Road, Auckland 10, New Zealand

First published 1977
Reprinted 1977, 1978, 1979, 1980
Second edition 1980
Reprinted 1981, 1982, 1983, 1985

Set, printed and bound in Great Britain by
Cox & Wyman Ltd, Reading
Set in Monotype Times

Contents

Preface to the Second Edition

My object in writing this book was to provide a brief summary of the competing approaches to the problem of inflation. Much of the academic literature on inflation is relatively abstruse and is not readily accessible to the general reader. With many issues of considerable technical complexity still to be resolved, economists have tended to shy away from presenting an overall account of the state of play between rival schools of thought which would be intelligible to non-professionals. This reluctance can in large measure be traced to a commendable dislike of the very real danger of over-simplification. Nevertheless with such a live issue as inflation, some attempt must be made to guide the non-specialist reader through this intellectual (and political) minefield. The non-specialist reader I had in mind when writing this book was someone not totally innocent of the elementary principles of economic analysis. For example, it would be a great advantage if the reader had some notion, however vague, of the points of difference between a Keynesian and a monetarist. It is hoped that this book will provide a useful supplement to an elementary course in economics, though many readers who are not engaged in the active study of economics may derive some benefit from it.

Fortunately within the last few years several texts have appeared which have attempted to provide a summary of the inflation literature with a lay audience in mind. Two excellent examples are *Inflation* by John Flemming (Oxford University Press) and *Inflation: The Price of Prosperity* by Brian Griffiths (Weidenfeld and Nicolson). The present book should be regarded not as a substitute but as a complement to the above texts. The interested reader is urged to consult the books by Flemming and Griffiths whenever he would like a different approach or a second opinion on a particular issue. The more advanced reader is advised to consult *The Economics of Inflation* by J.A. Trevithick and C. Mulvey (Martin Robertson) or 'Inflation: a survey' by David Laidler and Michael Parkin in the *Economic Journal*, December 1975.

Finally a comparison of this edition with the first edition will reveal that, although much of the basic analysis remains unaltered, the emphasis, particularly relating to economic policy, has shifted perceptibly. For example, a more favourable treatment of the cost-push school is mirrored in a more critical approach to the monetarist school. Hence my criticisms of monetarism can, in some degree, be levelled at my own earlier writings on the subject of inflation.

King's College,   JAMES TREVITHICK
Cambridge, January 1980

Chapter 1
Introduction: Facts and Theories

A Few Facts

In the last few years inflation has been accelerating at an alarming rate in most of the countries of the western bloc, to become for the first time by far their most pressing economic problem. That is not to say, of course, that for particular periods in particular countries inflation has not in the past posed a serious threat to national stability. One has simply to recall the disastrous consequences of the German hyper-inflation in 1923 to realize the havoc that inflation can wreak. Nevertheless the inflations which occurred before the Second World War could be seen to reflect some particular national crisis which *preceded* the fall in value of the currency. Expensive wars and their aftermath have traditionally been recognized as potent sources of inflationary pressure – the Korean and Vietnam wars are recent examples of this age-old phenomenon. Governments, in an attempt to squeeze more and more out of a hard-pressed wartime economy, have usually put excessive strain on the production capacity of the economy in their purchase of arms and equipment, the payment of troops, etc. Indeed wartime inflation, and the methods of avoiding or minimizing it, is the principal theme of Keynes's famous pamphlet *How to Pay for the War*. In an economy which is already fully stretched in producing the wherewithal to wage war effectively, the extra expenditure by the government simply serves to bid up the prices of the limited output of the economy. A *sustained* rise in expenditure by the government will, in such circumstances, lead to a *persistent* tendency for prices to rise, i.e. will lead to inflation.

It was generally assumed that once the economy returned to a more normal state of affairs, persistent inflation would disappear. Provided the economy was not subjected to any further external shock such as war or famine, and provided that the government acted in a responsible manner by refraining from putting undue strain on the productive capacity of the economy, the price level would remain more or less stable. However this should not be taken to imply that, abstracting from extraordinary events, prices *never* rose. One had to take account of a phenomenon known as the *trade* or *business* cycle. Prior to the Second World War, it was observed that capitalist economies were subject to regular patterns of expansion and contraction in the scale of output and hence in the level of employment. The upswing of a cycle corresponded to a period of rising output and falling unemployment and the downswing corresponded to falling output and rising unemployment. On the whole prices tended to move in sympathy with the general level of economic activity: in the upswing of the cycle prices would rise and in the downswing they would fall. The *trend rate of growth of prices* was roughly zero. The problem of *cyclical inflation* was therefore not regarded as being particularly serious.

The outbreak of the Second World War produced the persistent inflation which economists had come to associate with war. Indeed the inflation continued at a moderate rate right down to 1953 (the end of the Korean War) when an abatement of inflationary pressure was observed throughout the western world. Thenceforward inflation continued, but the annual rise in prices was of very modest, if not trifling, proportions by the standards of today. Although it cannot be said that rates of inflation of between 2 and 4 per cent per annum were welcomed with any enthusiasm, they were regarded as the price which had to be paid for full employment. Post-war politicians and economists, deeply influenced by J.M. Keynes's *General Theory of Employment, Interest and Money*, which had pinpointed the sources of widespread and prolonged unemployment, had come to regard the maintenance of full employment as the overriding objective of economic policy. To achieve this end they committed themselyes to a policy of continually stimulating spending whenever it appeared that unemployment might rise. A particularly favoured example of such a policy would be an expansion in the scale of public sector investment: the unemployed may be drawn into productive activity by being employed in public housing schemes, building roads, etc., on the deliberate initiative of the central government.

The point to be noted is that inflation, which had only been regarded as a transient occurrence before the war, had now come to be regarded as an integral part of the economic experience of mixed economies, i.e. economies where public and private enterprise exist side by side. So strong was the official attachment to full employment that the novel phenomenon of prolonged inflation was held to be an evil which had to be tolerated in order to mitigate the greater evil of widespread unemployment. Indeed there was (and is) a widespread belief among Keynesians that the commitment to full employment radically altered the rules of the capitalist game as far as the determination of money wages was concerned. For these Keynesians the adoption of a full employment policy required the simultaneous formulation of a wages policy: in circumstances where full employment was ensured by enlightened government action, the general level of money wages would, they feared, become a 'free' variable. Thus Joan Robinson (1971), echoing the words of Keynes, wrote: 'the general level of prices has become a political problem'.

The economic experience of the 1950s and most of the 1960s appeared to indicate that this attitude of resignation towards creeping inflation was paying off in terms of remarkably low unemployment rates and quite respectable growth rates (even in Britain). After 1967, however, events took a marked turn for the worse, as Table 1 indicates. For the first time in the post-war era, inflation showed a persistent tendency to *accelerate*. Moreover this acceleration of inflation was observed throughout the western trading bloc.

TABLE 1. *Average Rates of Inflation for Five Countries: 1953–66 and 1967–74*

	U.S.	U.K.	Germany	France	Japan
1953–66	1·48	3·4	2·23	3·94	3·86*
1967–74	5·36	7·5	4·27	6·48	7·51

* Source: *U.N. Statistical Yearbook*. Other sources: 1953–60, *The Problem of Rising Prices*, Fellner et al., OEEC, 1961; 1960–74, OECD, *Main Economic Indicators*.

With few exceptions, the rates of inflation of the non-Communist world reached alarming proportions, such as an annual rate of inflation of 23 per cent in Japan in 1974 and approximately 24 per cent in Britain early in 1975. What explanation have economists advanced for the disturbing acceleration in inflation? What remedies do they prescribe for its cure? In the chapters which follow we shall attempt to provide answers to these questions. But first a thumb-nail outline of some of the rival theories which have been proposed to explain inflation.

Theories

The problem of analysing the sources of inflationary pressure constitutes the major challenge to be faced by economic science in the 1980s. Just as the problem of massive unemployment severely called into question the established economic doctrine of the 1930s and ultimately led to the Keynesian revolution, so the alarming acceleration in the pace of inflation which has occurred throughout the western world since the end of the sixties has forced economists to re-examine and clarify their views on the forces which produce large fluctuations in the price level. In consequence the last few years have seen a veritable avalanche of specialist literature on the subject of inflation.

In our attempt to categorize the different approaches to the analysis of inflation, let us start with the two polar extremes, namely the *monetarist* and *cost-push* theories.

At one end of the spectrum there is the monetarist school of thought, which views inflation *exclusively* in terms of increases in the supply of money. Monetarists are impressed by what they regard as the conclusive evidence of history which indicates that all inflations of moderate duration are *caused by* increases in the size of the money stock. The classic example of the relation between monetary expansion and inflation is the inflow of gold and silver into Europe as a result of the Spanish conquest of the Americas. Another frequently quoted example is the inflation which occurred in Tudor England resulting, *inter alia*, from a good, old-fashioned debasement of the currency: once again, the inflation was due less to the diminished 'intrinsic' value of the debased coinage than to the increased number of coins in circulation. Similar arguments apply, say the monetarists, when the supply of money is determined, not by the availability of gold, but by the conduct of the central bank in managing the nation's currency. Though the day has long since passed when the supply of money was restricted by the quantity of gold that the central bank held as backing for the domestic currency, the same principles governing the relation between the price level and the supply of money still apply: price rises are only produced by the 'excess' issue of money by the central bank, probably acting under orders from the government. According to monetarists, therefore, inflation can only be brought under control by determined action by the government to restrict increases in the money supply.

At the other end of the spectrum are those who believe that the fundamental sources of inflationary pressure have nothing to do with basically economic factors, being primarily the result of sociological and political forces which, by implication, economics is incapable of analysing. According to this view, a much more fruitful line of inquiry consists, not in analysing the actions of the central bank or the Treasury, but in engaging in some form of sociological study of inter-class or inter-group conflict for increased shares in national income. The cost-push school maintains that a satisfactory understanding of the process of inflation cannot be obtained without a thorough study of the institutional framework within which wages and prices are determined. In particular they emphasize the dominant role that trade unions have come to play in most western economies in influencing the rate of wage increase, and hence the overall rate of inflation. Trade unions, it is argued, are not only in a position to coerce employers into yielding to their demands for higher wages, they are also able to put considerable pressure on governments to behave in similar fashion through the threat of an all-out strike.[1]

Moreover the influence of trade unions upon the pace of wage increase can be traced not merely to the struggle between employers, public or private, and workers, but also to an inter-union

1. In 1974, Mr Heath, the British Prime Minister, felt impelled to call a 'who governs the country' election as a counter to the miners' strike for higher pay, which ran directly against the statutory incomes policy then in force.

rivalry for what is perceived to be the 'just' rate of pay for one type of employment *vis-à-vis* another. What is a 'fair' differential between the wage of a bricklayer and that of a building labourer or, for that matter, a university teacher? If there is a general dissatisfaction with the existing pattern of wage differentials, some unions will attempt to 'leap-frog' over other unions in their wage claims, which will lead to retaliation and further attempted 'leap-frogging'. In other words inflation occurs when all of the claims by various groups in society for their 'fair' reward add up to more than the economy is capable of producing. Under such conditions the only thing that can 'give' is the price level.

As one may expect, there is enormous scope for variation within these two extreme positions. For example, the Keynesian position (or at least one version of the Keynesian position) recognizes the strength of changes in the supply of money in varying the level of aggregate spending but also recognizes that the power of trade unions may constitute an important impediment to an assault on inflation which relies on monetary restriction alone. Keynesians have found themselves in the hazardous cross-fire of the controversy between monetarists and cost-push theorists. Occupying the middle ground is never particularly healthy in a debate as highly charged as that on the causes of inflation. Eclectic Keynesians who eschew the dogmatic simplicities of the extreme positions can too easily be accused of pussy-footing and obfuscation.

Rival interpretations of the inflationary process lead to different recommendations for economic action to tackle inflation. The monetarists, quite naturally, advocate a policy of monetary control: all that is necessary is that the authorities in charge of the money supply should aim at producing a gradual but determined reduction in the rate of increase in the money supply (*how* this is done is explained in Chapter 6, page 90ff). They should adopt some target rate of increase in the supply of money roughly in line with the rate of increase in output (say 3–4 per cent in the case of Britain) and should then try to bring down the actual rate of monetary expansion so as to conform with this target figure. At the other extreme the cost-push theorists advocate policies which aim at a total reform of the institutions whereby wages and prices are determined. Many of this group favour a radical curtailment of the power sof trade unions and corporate monopolies, others the complete dismantling of the system of private enterprise and an end to the mixed economy. A policy of *permanent* control of prices and incomes is frequently mentioned with some approval.

In the chapters which follow, the broad lines of demarcation between the rival camps outlined above will be amplified. Although some of the differences of opinion and outlook between rival hypotheses can be traced to a large measure of verbal confusion, many issues of substance continue to divide writers on inflation and many of these can only be resolved by further empirical research. Indeed it is doubtful whether many of the competing theories regarding the sources of inflation can *ever* be verified by empirical methods alone. Ultimately the economist, even with the benefit of all the theories and their supporting evidence, will be forced into choosing one particular explanation, not on the basis of an absolutely clinching piece of empirical research, for none has yet emerged, but on the basis of his own intuition and perception of how the world works.

Predictably many commentators have attempted to attach political connotations to the differing views of the inflationary process. In particular they have tried to locate the monetarist school of thought on the extreme right wing of the political spectrum. Now while it is undoubtedly true that many, probably most, monetarists *do* have a bias in favour of allowing the market mechanism to function largely unimpeded by government meddling, it is also true that many economists who would broadly describe themselves as socialists have accepted the proposition that a régime of strict control over the growth in the money supply is necessary if inflation is to be conquered. This attempt to locate monetarism on the extreme political right becomes even more pointless when it is realized that most monetarists (certainly Professor Friedman – see Chapters 4 and 5) completely exonerate the trade union movement from any responsibility for inflation and oppose tooth and nail attempts to control by legislation the process of wage bargaining. Liberals and many neo-Keynesians, on the other hand, attribute much of the blame for the current inflation to the monopolistic practices of the trade union movement and advocate policies which, *inter alia*, will severely limit the exercise of trade union power. The picture becomes even more confused when one considers recent British experience: during the years 1972–4 the Conservative government ignored all of the standard monetarist nostra, allowing the money supply to grow at unprecedented rates. In contrast, the recent Labour government committed itself – admittedly under strong outside pressure – to bringing the growth in the money supply under control.

The moral of the story is that there is nothing *intrinsically* right wing in the monetarist remedy for inflation. One can believe in the complete socialization of the means of production and yet support policies to control the growth of the money supply. This said, however, if one were to conduct a head-count of those holding monetarist views one would tend to find a very high proportion who also believe in the virtues of the market mechanism and free enterprise.

In the chapters which follow a general picture of the state of play between the opposing schools of thought will be presented, in the hope that the reader will be tempted to formulate his own views regarding the causes of and the cures for the current inflation. An underlying theme of the later chapters is that the monetarists have greatly exaggerated the many apparent points of conflict between their own position and that of the Keynesians. In particular they claim, with scant textual justification, that the existence of a long-term Phillips curve (Chapter 4) constitutes an integral part of a Keynesian interpretation of inflation. But this is a highly misleading attribution by the monetarists. The Phillips curve was never part of Keynes's analytical structure and modern Keynesians – particularly the British branch of the family – have long been very suspicious of the whole notion of a 'trade off' between inflation and unemployment. The events of recent years seem, *prima facie*, to have vindicated this deeply rooted suspicion. Furthermore, the monetarists seem prone to gloss over the fact that certain forms of monetary expansion exert a more direct and immediate influence on aggregate spending than other forms, as Keynes came to recognize in his later writings.

Chapter 2
Pre-Keynesian Views on the Origins
of Inflation and Unemployment

For approximately 200 years before the publication of J.M. Keynes's *General Theory of Employment, Interest and Money* in 1936 there was broad agreement among writers on economic matters as to the sources of inflationary pressure. These economists tended to subscribe to one or other version of one of the most resilient theories in economics – *the quantity theory of money*. Associated with this theory are the names of Cantillon, Hume, Ricardo, J.S. Mill and Alfred Marshall: and, in our own century, of Pigou, Fisher and Hayek. Not surprisingly the apparent eclipse of Keynesian economics in recent years has been accompanied by a parallel revival of interest in the quantity theory of money. In particular the current vogue for monetarist explanations of inflation owes much to the reformulation of the quantity theory of money which was undertaken by Professor Milton Friedman and his colleagues at the University of Chicago in the 1950s. A knowledge of what older writers in the quantity-theory tradition had to say about the sources of price increases is therefore necessary to an understanding of the more sophisticated variations on a similar theme which have proliferated in the last couple of decades.

The Quantity Theory of Money

Let us start our inquiry into the characteristics of the quantity theory of money by assuming that we are dealing with a primitive economy which has no contacts with the outside world (and hence has no balance of payments problems), which produces only one commodity and which has only one means of payment, i.e. a commonly accepted instrument for settling debts of one sort or another between different individuals.

In order to simplify the problem we shall assume that the output of our hypothetical economy consists entirely of wheat and amounts to 200 bushels per annum. If we denote the output of the economy by the symbol Y, it follows that $Y = 200$ bushels. Now the output of the economy is not only the quantity of wheat which landowners and workers *produce* in a given year: it is also the amount of *real income* that they collectively *receive*, for *someone* must be in receipt of the produce of the land. In other words, 200 bushels of wheat accrue to landowners and workers in payment for the productive efforts. Economists therefore adopt the practice of identifying the *real income* of an economy with the *output* produced within the economy and of using these terms interchangeably.[1] Other things being equal, a higher income indicates the enjoyment of a higher standard of living for the whole population. For example, if, in consequence of an exceptionally favourable spell of good weather, the output of our economy were to rise from 200 bushels to 300 bushels, we would normally infer that the welfare of the inhabitants of the economy had also improved.[2]

As a further simplification we shall assume that the means of payment referred to above consists solely of gold coin of a certain quality. The existence of this readily acceptable means of payment greatly improves the efficiency of the process of exchanging one good for another and is the hallmark of a *money-using* economy as compared to a *barter* economy. Let there be 100 coins circulating in the economy and let each coin be labelled 'one pound'. If we denote the supply of gold by the symbol M, it follows that $M = £100$. Moreover since economists define the *supply of money* as any generally accepted means of settling debt, we quite naturally deduce that the money supply has but one single

1. Complications arise when taxation, foreign trade and the replacement of capital equipment are brought into the picture.

2. Not all economists would accept that an increase in the volume of output is necessarily beneficial to society. Considerations of ecology, for example, may indicate that certain forms of productive activity are positively harmful to general welfare. We shall ignore these factors since they are not really germane to the main theme of this book.

18

component in our hypothetical economy, viz. £100 worth of gold coin.

The question to which quantity theorists now turn is: Given the supply of money (£100) and the level of real income (200 bushels of wheat), what will determine the price level, which we shall label P, at which each bushel will sell? By extension they also ask: What factors will lead to a *change* in the price level? In order to furnish satisfactory answers to these questions, it is customary to introduce the equation of exchange made famous by Professor Irving Fisher.

Fisher's Equation of Exchange

Let us consider a modified[3] version of this, expressed symbolically as follows:

$$MV = PY \text{ (i.e. money supply times V equals price level times real income)}$$

The only symbol which as yet is unexplained is the symbol V, the *velocity of circulation of money*: V is the average number of times that £1 changes hands in purchasing the output of the economy in, say, one year. Workers and the other agents in the productive process are paid in the form of money. Yet money, in itself, is only useful to the extent that it can be exchanged for the fruits of their collective labour, viz. the total output of the economy. The frequency with which £1 passes through the hands of a 'representative' individual is its velocity of circulation.

If the velocity of circulation of money is, for example, 24, then an examination of the equation of exchange reveals that the price of a bushel of wheat will be £12. That is, since M = £100, V = 24 and Y = 200, it follows that P = £12. Hence if we know M, V and Y, Fisher's equation enables us to isolate the determinants of the general price level. Furthermore it predicts that, if V and Y remain constant (see below), then a necessary and sufficient condition for an increase in the price level is an increase in the supply of money.

3. It is modified in the sense that whereas Fisher was interested in the amount of money changing hands in *all* transactions, including intermediate transactions, we are more concerned with transactions which involve the purchase of the *final* output of the economy.

For example, a doubling in the supply of gold will lead to a similar doubling in the price level.

In the past the equation of exchange has come in for considerable criticism, not on the grounds that it is untrue, but simply because it in no way imparts relevant information as to how the world works. The equation of exchange has often been denounced as an identity, a truism which serves no useful purpose. In order to understand the arguments underlying this criticism, let us compare the components on each side of the equation of exchange. The left-hand side of the equation, MV, is simply the total amount of money spent *on* the output of the economy while the right-hand side, PY, is the total *value* of that output. According to these critics, Fisher's equation is a mere tautology, for it states the trivial commonplace that the amount spent on wheat by the consumers of wheat is always, without exception, equal to the money income of the producers of that wheat. It merely restates the dual nature of all transactions, namely that the amount of a commodity bought will always, by definition, be equal to the amount sold. While one man's expenditure is another man's income, the expenditure of the *whole* economy is its *own* income. Why, then, has the quantity theory of money exerted such a powerful influence on the development of economic analysis? If it is a mere tautology, how can it be regarded as an *explanation* of the phenomenon of inflation? The answer is that Fisher's equation of exchange must first of all have certain restrictions placed upon it before it can be viewed as an explanation of anything.

Two Restrictions on Fisher's Equation of Exchange

The first assumption that quantity theorists made was that the level of output (equal to the level of real income) in the economy is *independent of the size of the money stock*. If, for example, the quantity of money circulating in the economy were to double from £100 to £200 worth of gold coin, the level of output, in the long run at least, will remain unaffected. True, most quantity theorists have argued that output and trade may be stimulated for a short period as a result of expansions in the supply of money; but they always emphasized the transient nature of this phenomenon. In the long run, an increase in the money stock would not alter the basic ability of an economy to produce goods and services. The productive potential of the economy was determined at its *full employment level* (see below) by non-monetary factors such as the size and skills of the working population, the sex and age mix, attitudes towards work, etc.; upon the quantity and productivity of the capital equipment employed in the process of production; and upon the efficiency with which capital, labour and other inputs into the productive process were combined. The level of output is therefore determined by 'real' as opposed to 'monetary' factors. To use Pigou's famous phrase, money is simply a veil behind which the more fundamental economic forces operate according to the time-honoured principles of supply and demand.

The second assumption is the proposition that the income velocity of circulation of money, V, is, to all intents and purposes, constant. Quantity theorists rarely went so far as to maintain that V was *always* constant, or that it would not be subject to changed economic circumstances. For example, it was often recognized that during periods of inflation individuals would develop a certain reluctance to hold money and would tend to re-circulate it more rapidly. Money burns a larger hole in one's pocket when the rate of inflation is 50 per cent than when it is 5 per cent because of the more rapid rate of decline of its purchasing power. An increase in the rate of inflation could therefore put upward pressure on velocity. Moreover it was also conceded that, as the financial infrastructure of advancing economies became more and more complex and specialized, the need to hold money for transaction purposes might diminish progressively.

Nevertheless, although both short- and long run factors could exert an influence upon V, little importance was attached to them: short-term fluctuations in V were regarded as exceptional and shortlived whilst long-term changes in V manifested themselves over a sufficiently extended period of time as to be negligible as far as the analysis of particular situations was concerned.

The Cambridge Equation

An alternative and, in many ways, more satisfactory formulation of the quantity theory of money is contained in the *Cambridge equation*. As its name indicates, this approach to the quantity theory of money was pioneered at Cambridge University in the early years of this century and is principally associated with the name of Alfred Marshall. The Cambridge equation may be expressed symbolically as follows:

$$M = kPY$$

Once again M, P and Y need no further explanation. The novel component of this equation is what has come to be known as the 'Cambridge k' which we shall see shortly is simply the reciprocal of Fisher's V (i.e. $k = \dfrac{1}{V}$).

But why should the Cambridge formulation of the quantity theory of money be regarded as superior to Fisher's? After all, is it not merely an arithmetical reshuffling of his equation of exchange? The answer to this question can be found in the manner in which Cambridge theorists considered the holding of money as the outcome of *rational choice*. They asked themselves: Why do people hold money? That is, what will be the most important determinants of the *demand for money*? They postulated that the most important factor which influenced the amount of money individuals wish to hold is the level of *money income*, i.e. PY.

The reasoning behind this hypothesis is briefly this. We live in a money-using economy in which individuals not only receive their incomes through the medium of money but also effect transactions through the exchange of money. However the individual receives his income at discrete intervals (normally weekly or monthly) but has to pay for certain items more or less continuously. For example, an office-worker who receives his salary on a monthly basis still has to pay for his lunch, his train fare and his daily pint(s) of beer, etc., on a daily basis. In other words an individual must make provision for everyday expenditure out of his money income which he receives in a more discontinuous, though nevertheless regular, pattern. If the individual is paid monthly, his holding of money at the beginning of the month will equal the entire amount of his salary and (assuming he is not saving) his holding of money at the end of the month will be zero. If he spends his income at a uniform rate throughout the month, his average holding of money will equal one half of his monthly income. Moreover if we examine his average holding of money *over the whole year*, we will also find that it is roughly one half of his monthly salary or $\frac{1}{24}$ of his annual income. Now if *all* individuals behaved in exactly the same manner as our exemplary individual, we would necessarily deduce that the Cambridge k, which is simply the demand for money balances, M divided into the level of money income, PY, was also around $\frac{1}{24}$. That is, $M = \frac{1}{24} PY$.

According to the Cambridge equation, the demand for money will be a fairly constant proportion of the level of money income. As money incomes rise, the necessity to hold larger cash balances to finance a correspondingly higher volume of money expenditure will rise *pari passu*. Cambridge theorists followed the example set by Fisher in assuming (a) that the level of real income is, in the longer term, determined by 'real' factors and (b) that the average value of k would be unlikely to change much over the short to medium period and that changes which manifest themselves over a longer period can be taken account of without much difficulty.

The Fundamental Prediction of the Quantity Theory of Money

Whichever formulation of the quantity theory of money is selected, the fact remains that once we have imposed the restriction on V (or k) and Y outlined above, we have transformed what was a mere tautology into a behavioural relationship capable of forward prediction. The central prognostication of the quantity theory of money may now be advanced, viz. that an increase in the quantity of money will lead to an *equiproportionate increase* in the price level. In our example, if the quantity of money circulating in the economy doubled from £100 to £200, the price of a bushel of wheat (the only commodity produced in our deliberately rudimentary economy) would also double from £12 to £24. The real income of the economy, 200 bushels of wheat, would remain unchanged. However *money* incomes would double on account of the doubling of prices. It should also be noted that quantity theorists did not confine price increases to a change in the value of final output (wheat). The prices of all inputs into the productive process would increase by exactly the same proportion. For example, a doubling of the size of the money stock would also double *money* wages. *Real* wages, however, would remain unaffected on account of the fact that the increase in the money wage would be exactly offset by the increase in the price of wheat. The wage-earner can only buy exactly the same quantity of wheat with his wage packet as before.

Thus a quantity theorist views increases in the absolute price level, P, as being solely the outcome of prior increases in the quantity of money in circulation, M. They regard as incontrovertible the testimony of history which shows that from the time of the Emperor Diocletian down to the present day, substantial increases in the price level have almost always been associated with increases in the supply of money. Before about 1750, increases in M came about mainly through the discovery of new gold or silver mines, or through the depredations of war. In more recent years, increases in the money stock have principally resulted from the actions of the central bank (in the United States the Federal Reserve Board, in Britain the Bank of England) which acts at one remove from the government. Occasionally it was recognized that certain natural or man-made disasters such as poor harvests or wars could cause increases in prices in that, if output fell relative to the stock of money, Fisher's equation implies a rise in the price level for a constant velocity of circulation. For the majority of cases, however, the motive force behind the increases in P was an increase in M. Finally, since inflation is the phenomenon of persistently rising prices, the quantity theorist regards continual increases in the money supply as being the principal cause of inflation.

At this stage the reader should be warned that the historical evidence is not nearly as unambiguous as the monetarists appear to believe. True, most economic historians agree that, before 1900 (or perhaps even before 1939), the inflations that occurred could be attributed to some excess of aggregate demand over aggregate supply. However, this broad consensus breaks down when it comes to analysing the sources of excess aggregate demand during particular inflationary periods. Considerable controversy has raged over whether demand-side (monetary) or supply-side disturbances were principally responsible for upward pressures on the price level. To take but one example: the traditional explanation of the Price Revolution in sixteenth-century Europe – if one can call a 'revolution' a rate of inflation averaging between 1 and 2 per cent – accords pride of place to the enormous expansion in the world supply of gold and silver resulting from the Spanish conquest of the Caribbean and South and Central America. This monetarist perspective on the Price Revolution held sway for many centuries: observers from Jean Bodin in the 1560s to Friedman in the 1970s (and including Keynes in his *Treatise on Money*, 1930) have lent their support to this plausible view. But on further scrutiny of the rather fragmentary evidence, some economic historians have placed much greater emphasis on supply-side factors such as the large population increases in most European countries coupled with diminishing returns, particularly in agriculture.

But even this hypothesis must remain speculative since pre-nineteenth-century economic history is bedevilled by the paucity of reliable statistics. Referring to the rival explanations of the Price Revolution, one eminent historian has observed that 'there is as little hard evidence on the rate of population growth as there is on the money supply' (Phyllis Deane, 1979). So the testimony of history should be handled very gingerly: Friedman's famous quip that 'inflation is always and everywhere a monetary phenomenon' would be regarded by most economic historians as at best unproven and at worst empirically groundless.

The Necessity of Money

At this stage a word of warning should be sounded. It is the quantity-theory view that the standard of living of the economy would not be affected either adversely or favourably by an isolated increase in the quantity of money. Admittedly money variables such as the money wage rate and the price level would change, but real variables, such as the level of real income and the real wage rate, would remain the same. To this extent money is a veil, concealing the more fundamental forces which determine the standard of life of the economy.

Nevertheless it should not be deduced that money serves no useful purpose in an economy. It has long been recognized that the *existence* of a widely accepted means of exchange (e.g. gold; pound

25

notes, dollar bills and other forms of 'managed' money) greatly improves the efficiency of exchange. As we have said above, an economy with a well-established means of exchange will be considerably more efficient than its polar opposite, a barter economy. The commercial superiority of a money-using economy over economies where barter is the standard form of trading is well known. Quantity theorists would be the last to deny this superiority. What they argue is that once an economy has developed a means of exchange which is accepted for the vast majority of commercial transactions, and once patterns of production and exchange have adapted themselves to the more specialized form of trading which the introduction of money makes possible, an *increase* in the quantity of money will not affect these patterns. If money is the lubricant of the system of exchange, it has the property that a drop will serve just as well as a poolful.

The Monetary Transmission Mechanism

Up to this point all that we have demonstrated is that, if V and Y are judged to be constant, an increase in the supply of money *must* produce an equiproportionate increase in prices. Now it is one thing to grasp this arithmetical necessity: it is quite another to appreciate how the increase in M *produces* the rise in P. What we want to know is the precise mechanism through which an increase in the money stock generates rises in the price level.

At this stage of the discussion we cannot go into a detailed treatment of the transmission mechanisms whereby the price level is supposed to be affected by monetary stimuli. In what follows a rudimentary outline of just one of the many mechanisms will be sketched. This mechanism has come to be known as the *cash-balance* mechanism, although we shall see later on when discussing the appropriate definition of the money supply that this is something of a misnomer in that cash is but one part, and a very small part at that, of the total supply of money. The cash-balance mechanism states that when individuals find themselves with an excessive supply of money in relation to their money income, their reaction will be to *spend the excess*. Consider the Cambridge equation and remember that it is essentially a theory of the *demand* for money. For a given level of money income, individuals will have a given demand for money. We can therefore write $M^d = kPY$ where the superscript d denotes the demand for money. The *supply* of money on the other hand will be denoted by M^s.

A vital assumption in the quantity-theory interpretation of inflation is that the supply of money is determined by a set of factors which are independent of the factors which determine the demand for it. For example, in a system where the supply of money consists solely of gold coin, M^s will be primarily determined by the output of gold from the mines of that economy or some other economy. It will not be 'determined' by the level of money income, though high prices for gold itself will clearly encourage the more vigorous exploitation of existing workings.

The question now arises: Through what channel does the supply of money increase? In a monetary system dominated by gold, an increase in the supply of money could be the result of the discovery of new mine workings. In more advanced systems, it could be the result of the government spending more than it receives either from tax revenues or from borrowing from the public, the financing of this excess expenditure taking the form of 'borrowing from the banking system' (a process often described – inaccurately – as 'printing money'). More specifically M^s will exceed M^d. For as long as the positive discrepancy between M^s and M^d persists, individuals will be dissatisfied with the amount of money they are holding, preferring instead to buy commodities[4] with the surplus money balances. Since the supply of commodities is already given by real factors, discussed in greater detail in the following section, any attempt by individuals to purchase more than is currently being produced within the economy will simply bid up the prices of the commodities.

4. In a more complete model, individuals would also tend to purchase physical and financial assets. Indeed Keynes maintained that the most important repercussions of an increase in M^s would be to increase the issue of financial assets, the production of commodities being relatively insensitive to such an increase. Nevertheless he recognized that *some* forms of monetary increase could exert a powerfully stimulating effect on the purchase of commodities. See Chapter 6.

In our example the initial supply of money is £100. Since this is also equal to the demand for money when the price of wheat is £12, we infer that £12 is the price level which will equate the supply of and demand for money. A doubling of the supply of money to £200 generates a discrepancy between M^s and M^d. Individuals only *wish* to hold £100 worth of money ($\frac{1}{24}$th of the value of the money income) whereas the amount of money *actually* in circulation is £200. The collective response of economic agents is to *attempt* to purchase more wheat. But since the full-employment output of wheat is fixed at 200 bushels, increased expenditure on wheat can only result in a higher price. The rise in the price of wheat will continue until individuals, on balance, cease to attempt to 'offload' money. This in turn will occur only when the price level has risen by a sufficient amount (to £24 per bushel) to produce a level of money income where £200 is the quantity of money which individuals wish to hold in relation to their money incomes. In other words money income will rise to a level where £200 is exactly $\frac{1}{24}$th of the value of money income, for only at that level will M^s equal M^d. To satisfy the Cambridge equation (or equivalently Fisher's equation), P must rise to a level where $£200 = \frac{1}{24} \times P \times 200$. Rearrangement reveals that P must rise to £24.

The Classical Theory of Output and Employment: the Assumption of Full Employment

We have said that quantity theorists regarded the level of real income, Y, as being fixed by a set of relations which are independent of the size of the money stock. In fact, however, they went much further than this. They asserted that, in a competitive economy where wages and prices are free to fluctuate in response to market pressures, there would be an *automatic* tendency for full employment to be established. This is a cardinal tenet of classical economics, of which the quantity theory of money is only a part, albeit a very important part.

Unemployment and the Labour Market

In order to grasp the logic of this proposition, certain heroic and, the reader may think, unrealistic assumptions must be made. Let us assume that we can treat the whole of the labour market as one large, homogeneous entity so that we can speak of *the* labour market, *the* demand for labour, *the* supply of labour, etc. Once this step has been taken we can then analyse the labour market in the same way as we would analyse the behaviour of any other market, investigating the factors which determine the demand for and supply of labour.

Let us consider the demand for labour first. At its simplest, classical theory states that the lower the cost of employing labour, the more labour will be employed. Employers will compare the money wage rate to the price at which they can sell their output and, on the basis of this calculation, will decide how much labour to employ. Clearly a reduction in the money wage rate (the money cost of employing labour) relative to the price of his output will make it profitable for the employer to take on more labour. Stated more concisely, progressive reductions in the *real wage rate* would be matched by corresponding increases in the demand for labour. The theoretical justification for this hypothesis is to be found in what is called the *marginal productivity theory of wages*. This theory is based on two assumptions: (a) that as the employment of labour is steadily increased, each successive unit of labour will add less to total output than the preceding one – this is the principle of diminishing returns applied to the labour market; (b) that profit-maximizing employers, faced with an arbitrarily given real wage rate, will employ labour up to the point at which the marginal product of labour[5] is exactly equal to that real wage rate. It follows that a reduction in the real wage rate will induce the representative employer to hire more labour in order to maintain equality between the real wage rate and the marginal product of labour. The demand for labour function can therefore be represented by the L^d curve in Figure 1.

In Figure 1, w stands for the real wage rate, L^d for the demand for labour and L^s for the supply of labour. We are following the

5. It should be noted that when we refer to the marginal product of labour, we are implicitly assuming that both the size of the capital stock and the techniques of production being employed are not changing over the period under consideration. This is the standard convention of both classical and Keynesian short-run analysis.

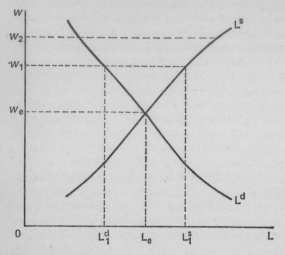

Figure 1

practice of classical economists in being less explicit concerning the shape of the *supply* of labour curve. By the way we have drawn the curve, we have assumed that the supply of labour will increase as the real wage rate rises. That is, the number of men offering themselves for employment – or the number of hours that each man is willing to work – will be an increasing function of the real wage rate. But this is by no means a necessary assumption. The essential characteristics of the classical theory of employment are not appreciably altered if the assumption is made that the L^s curve is vertical, or even that it has a *negative* slope. Nevertheless we shall assume for the sake of argument that the supply of labour function depicted in Figure 1 is an accurate representation of supply conditions in the labour market.

Suppose now that, for whatever reason, the economic system 'inherited' a real wage rate w_1. The supply of labour is L_1^s while the demand for labour is only L_1^d. The number of men offering themselves for employment considerably exceeds the number of men actually being hired by employers, which is just another way of saying that substantial unemployment exists. According to classical economists, the origins of this sort of unemployment can be traced to the prevalence of excessively high real wages. Moreover in a freely functioning market economy this unemployment can only be a temporary phenomenon. The existence of an excess supply of labour will lead to a competitive struggle between employed and unemployed workers for the limited number of jobs available. Unemployed workers will attempt to undercut employed workers by offering themselves for work at a lower real wage rate. Gradually, as the real wage rate falls, the employment of labour rises and the discrepancy between the supply of and demand for labour diminishes. Unemployment will ultimately disappear[6] once the wage rate has been driven down to w_e. The establishment of a real wage rate w_e will produce a situation of what economists call *labour-market clearance*. This particular real wage rate is at once the *equilibrium* and *full-employment* real wage rate: no distinction is made between the two. The level of employment will eventually converge upon L_e, the equilibrium level of employment.

What, then, are the sources of unemployment in classical economics? The answer appears to be fairly simple: excessively high real wages, i.e. real wages in excess of w_e. But if, as classical economists believed, the market were allowed to operate freely, large-scale unemployment could not persist for very long. If widespread unemployment *did* persist over long periods, then the origins of this unemployment had to be traced to factors which impeded the functioning of the market mechanism. In particular, attention has to be focused on monopolistic elements in the labour market which, by resisting money wage cuts, prevented the re-establishment of full employment. These monopolistic elements were, predictably, trade unions which, as monopoly suppliers of labour, were in a strong position to 'price labour out of the market'.

This was the received explanation of persistent unemployment:

6. Once again this is not strictly true. There could still be *some* unemployment even at a wage rate w_e. This would be exclusively *frictional* unemployment, i.e. the unemployment which results from workers voluntarily leaving their current jobs in order to seek alternative employment and registering as unemployed during this interim period between resignation and re-employment.

if an economic phenomenon endured for longer than the period of the normal trade cycle it was to be analysed in terms of the classical theory of relative prices. However there was another, less well-defined area of economic speculation: the theory of the business or trade cycle. It was recognized by classical writers that capitalist economies were prone to fluctuations in activity around long-term trends and that these fluctuations exhibited a fairly regular pattern of behaviour. In an upswing, output, employment and prices tended to rise and in a downswing they tended to fall. Nonetheless the classical authors, lacking an adequate theory of effective demand (see Chapter 3), were unable to integrate the theory of the business cycle into their vision of how a market economy would develop in the long run.

The Relation between Employment and Output:
The Short-Run Production Function

When we analysed the factors influencing the demand for labour, we indicated that, as the real wage rate fell, the demand for labour would rise. But reductions in the real wage rate not only stimulate[7] the level of employment, they also raise the level of output. The increased level of employment made possible by the lower real wage rate also enables employers to raise the level of production. For a given outlay on labour, employers will be able to take on more men at the lower real wage rate; since each of the additional men produces extra output, albeit at a progressively diminishing rate, total output will rise.

We may depict this phenomenon diagrammatically in Figure 2. This relation between the level of employment and the level of output is summarized in a curve known as the *short-run production function*. (It is short-run in the sense that the capital stock and techniques of production are assumed to be unchanged over the period under study.) The significance of the relation is quite easy to grasp and needs little elaboration. As more labour is employed in the productive process, the volume of output will rise. Thus the economy is capable of producing more output (Y_2) when the employment of labour is L_2 than when it is L_1. Moreover since

7. We are, of course, implicitly assuming that w is falling from a level in excess of w_e, e.g. from a level w_1.

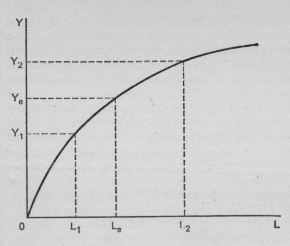

Figure 2. The Short-Run Production Function

we already know from our analysis of the labour market that there are automatic forces which will continually push the level of employment to L_e, we are able to deduce from the production function that the level of output will be Y_e at this point. This level of output will also be the *full-employment level of real income* since it corresponds to a level of employment L_e. In an ideal classical world, therefore, real income will be continually hovering around its full employment level.

Summary

From the preceding account of the classical theory of output, employment and prices, several important propositions emerge:

(1) The levels of output and employment are determined by the real forces of supply and demand which operate behind the veil of money.

(2) In a freely functioning market economy, prolonged unemployment cannot occur since real wages will adjust in such a way as to ensure the maintenance of continual full employment. An excess supply of labour will therefore result in downward pressure

33

on the real wage rate. Once the real wage rate has adjusted so as to clear the labour market (i.e. equate the supply of and demand for labour), the level of real income (= output) will settle down at its full employment level, Y_e. As we have seen, the independent determination of the level of real income is an integral part of the quantity theory of money.

(3) A corollary of (2) is that prolonged unemployment can only be explained in terms of monopolistic impediments which hinder the operation of the market mechanism. For example, trade unions, as monopoly suppliers of labour, were often regarded as one of the forces which prevented the real wage rate from falling to its full employment level, w_e.

(4) Though no classical economist ever maintained that the velocity of circulation of money was an immutable constant, there was a general belief that it was highly stable and was only susceptible to very minor change in the short to medium period.

(5) It follows from propositions (1)–(4) that the price level is exclusively determined by the size of the money supply. Moreover increases in the money supply produce equiproportionate increases in the price level. An increase in the supply of money of x per cent produces an increase in the price level of x per cent. In other words, the rate of inflation (the rate of increase in the price level) will equal the rate of monetary expansion (the rate of increase in the money supply).

Chapter 3
Keynesianism

Keynes and the Principle of Effective Demand

The experience of massive and prolonged unemployment in Britain and, to a lesser extent, in the other nations of the western world during the inter-war period cast a long shadow over the whole of the classical system. The self-righting properties of classical economics were clearly not working. The real wage rate did not fall and widespread unemployment refused to go away. Although many earlier economists had hinted at the sources of this unemployment, Keynes was the first writer to produce a unified, coherent and theoretically convincing explanation of the inter-war unemployment.

Keynes traced the sources of unemployment to a *deficiency of effective demand*. Stated crudely, his theory amounted to the proposition that economic agents, considered collectively, were not spending enough on the output of the economy to employ fully the available labour force. If only economic agents could be induced to *spend* more, output would rise, leading to a rise in employment. According to Keynes's theory, the level of output is determined by the effective demand for that output.

In his simplified treatment of the composition of effective demand, Keynes distinguished between two separate elements: consumption (C) and investment (I). Effective demand (E) is the sum of the amount spent on consumer goods and services and the amount spent on investment goods, i.e. E = C + I. So let us examine each of the components of effective demand in turn.

1. The Consumption and Saving Functions

Keynes postulated that the amount spent on consumption goods would principally depend upon the level of real income accruing to

35

individuals as a whole. As real income rises, the amount spent on consumption goods will also rise. The notion that, as they become better off, individuals spend more on consumer goods can hardly be regarded as trail-blazing, but we shall see below that it came to play a central role in Keynes's theory of the determinants of output and employment, and hence in his diagnosis of the sources of unemployment.

Keynes, having stated that there would be some positive association between the level of consumption and the level of real income which he called the *consumption function*, did not stop at that. He maintained that each successive increment to real income would be matched by a *smaller* increment to consumption expenditure, the remainder being diverted into savings. Consider a consumption function such as the one depicted in Figure 3.

Consumption and saving are measured on the vertical axis and real income, Y, on the horizontal. Suppose now that the economy's real income were £400m. and that, of that £400m., £350m. took

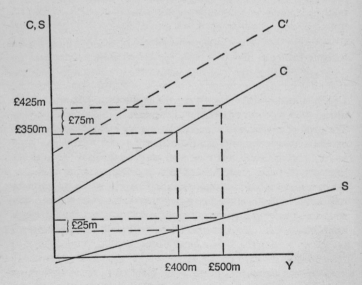

Figure 3. The Consumption Function

the form of the production of and expenditure on consumer goods. What would happen to consumption expenditure if, for reasons that will become apparent below, real income rose from £400m. to £500m.? The answer is that consumption would rise, but by an amount *less* than the £100m. increase in income. Suppose, for example, that for each £100m. increase in income, consumption expenditure rose by only £75m., the remaining £25m. being saved. The *marginal propensity to consume*, which is defined as the ratio of the increase in consumption expenditure to the increase in income, would then be 0.75 $\left(\text{i.e.} \dfrac{£75\text{m.}}{£100\text{m.}} \right)$. The *marginal propensity to save*, defined similarly, would be 0.25 $\left(\dfrac{£25\text{m.}}{£100\text{m.}} \right)$. Three quarters of each increase in real income will be devoted to greater consumption, the remaining quarter being siphoned off into higher savings. Hence we can also construct a *saving function* since saving is an increasing function of income (provided, of course, that the marginal propensity to consume is less than unity). The fact that not all of an increase in income is absorbed into a higher level of consumption but is partly channelled into higher savings plays an important part in Keynes's theory of employment.

2. Investment

Unlike consumption, investment was regarded by Keynes to be determined by factors largely independent of the level of income. The level of investment expenditure is principally determined (a) by the long-term state of confidence in the future profitability of investment projects; and (b) by the rate of interest. Determinant (a), what Keynes called 'the state of long-term expectation', borders on a truism: obviously entrepreneurs will be less inclined to risk their capital when there is a great deal of uncertainty surrounding the future profitability of investment projects. Determinant (b), the rate of interest, occupies a central position in Keynes's theory of investment. For a given state of business confidence, a reduction in the rate of interest will encourage entrepreneurs to invest in a wider variety of projects. The lower cost of borrowing capital (the rate of interest) relative to the future stream of income on investment projects enables the entrepreneur to invest money in projects which would have been unprofitable at a higher interest rate owing to the higher cost of capital.

Although the behaviour of the rate of interest becomes vitally important in our discussion of monetary policy in Chapter 6, we shall for the moment assume that it is constant. By inference we are assuming that the level of investment expenditure, I, is also constant.

Effective Demand and the Level of Real Income

Clearly the amount spent on goods and services must equal the amount of those goods and services which are actually sold. This is, once again, a mere tautology, similar to the one discussed in relation to Fisher's equation. What is not a tautology is the proposition that the volume of production (i.e. the level of real income) will *adapt itself* to variations in the sale of goods and services. This last sentence provides an important clue to the nature of Keynesian equilibrium: real income will be at its *equilibrium* level when the volume of output has accommodated itself to the existing demand for goods and services. In other words, equilibrium prevails when the output of producers has expanded or contracted by a sufficient amount to be just equal to the amount that consumers and investors are willing to spend on their output.

This proposition, considered radical in its day, is far from being self-evident and stands in need of some explanation. Consider Figure 4. Total expenditure, that is the sum of consumption expenditure and investment expenditure, is measured on the vertical axis and real income on the horizontal. When discussing the determinants of the level of investment we said that it would remain constant (a) if the state of business confidence remained unchanged, and (b) if the rate of interest did not vary. For the moment we shall assume that conditions (a) and (b) hold good so that, to all intents and purposes, the level of investment is also constant. Since investment is constant, it does not change as the level of income changes, i.e. the level of investment can be represented by the horizontal line I in Figure 4.

In contrast, the other component of expenditure, consumption, *does* vary with the level of income since the consumption function

38

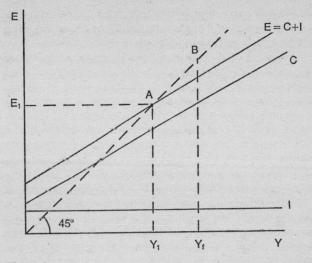

Figure 4

has a positive slope. If we add these two components of expenditure together and represent the sum on a diagram we obtain the *total-expenditure function*, which shows how the total amount of money spent on the output of the economy itself varies with that output. In Figure 4, the total-expenditure function is given by the line $E = C + I$. Since we have assumed that I is invariant with the level of real income for the reasons outlined above, it is clear that the only reason why the total-expenditure function slopes upwards is that consumption (the more important component of expenditure) rises as income rises. Indeed, inspection of the diagram reveals that the total-expenditure function is *parallel* to the consumption function: a given increase in income, by producing an increment in consumption expenditure (but not in investment), will produce an equal increment in total expenditure. In Keynesian terminology, the marginal propensity to *spend*[1] will equal the marginal propensity to consume, the marginal propensity to invest being zero by assumption.

1. That is, the increase in spending resulting from a unit increase in income.

Finally we must discuss the dotted line in Figure 4. This is often referred to as the 45° line since, as its name implies, it bisects an angle of 90°. The significance of this line resides, however, not in its trigonometric properties, but in the fact that, if national income is to be in equilibrium, income must equal expenditure. In other words, equilibrium can only prevail when the amount that individuals are willing to *spend* on the output of the economy (E) is equal to the amount of output that entrepreneurs are willing to *produce* (Y). Now it is perfectly possible for Y to exceed E for brief periods, that is for entrepreneurs to produce more than consumers and investors are collectively willing to spend. But in this case, entrepreneurs will simply be accumulating unsold stocks of unwanted output and will react by cutting back on the scale of production until they are producing just that volume of output that they can sell to purchasers. That is, the scale of output will accommodate itself to the level of expenditure. Herein lies the significance of the 45° line – it is only along this line that the amount that consumers and investors are collectively willing to spend is equal to the amount that entrepreneurs are willing to produce.

But the question now arises: At what point along the 45° line will the economy eventually settle? The answer is: At the point where the total-expenditure function intersects with the 45° line (point A in Figure 4). The *equilibrium* level of income and expenditure will be Y_1 and E_1 respectively. Were Y to exceed Y_1 there would be unsold and unwanted stocks of output in the hands of producers who would then cut back on production. If, on the other hand, Y fell short of Y_1, stocks of goods would soon run out, shortages would develop and production would expand. Only at point A, the point of intersection of the total-expenditure function with the 45° line, will the expenditure plans of consumers and investors be consistent with the production plans of entrepreneurs. In short, the level of real income is determined by the position of the total-expenditure function.

Effective Demand and Unemployment

In order to illustrate how Keynes's principle of effective demand can be used to explain the phenomenon of unemployment, let us assume that the economy starts off in a position of full employment (see Figure 1, page 30). The number of men offering themselves for employment equals the number of men actually being taken on by employers. Let us re-label the level of output which would be necessary to sustain this level of employment Y_f, in order to emphasize that we are referring to the *full employment level of output*.

We saw in our discussion of the classical system that, if the actual level of output were to fall persistently short of Y_f, then the origins of this discrepancy were to be found in market imperfections of some sort, in particular imperfections in the labour market arising from the power of trade unions. Keynes's achievement was to point to a completely different source for such unemployment. Unemployment was due to a lack of effective demand: the expenditure plans of consumers and investors, when considered together, were simply insufficient to produce a level of output which would employ the whole of the available labour force. Referring back to Figure 4, the position of the total-expenditure function, E_1, indicates that output will settle down at a level where a considerable proportion of the labour force will be unemployed. Unemployment can only be eliminated if steps are taken to *raise* the expenditure function to a position where it intersects with the 45° line at point B. In terms of our simple model this can be achieved by raising either the level of consumption expenditure or the level of investment. Precisely *how* these components of effective demand can be raised is the subject of the following subsection.

Fiscal Policy as an Instrument of Demand Management

If one accepts the Keynesian diagnosis of the source of unemployment, viz. that it is the result of a deficiency of aggregate expenditure, then it is but a short step to prescribing policies which raise the level of aggregate demand as a cure for unemployment. In terms of a simple Keynesian model, this can be achieved in two ways: either by raising the level of government expenditure, G, to augment private investment; or by reducing the general level of taxation in order to stimulate consumer expenditure. Both types of policy come under the general heading of *fiscal* policy. Fiscal policy is the deliberate manipulation of the size of the government budget deficit (i.e. the difference between the amount it spends and the amount it collects in taxes) in order to achieve some economic objective such as higher employment or lower inflation.

Let us take the most frequently cited example of an expansionary fiscal policy – an increase in government spending. It is well known that, throughout the 1930s, Keynes, along with many other Cambridge economists, advocated a policy of deliberately unbalancing the budget by undertaking public work schemes such as building houses. For our purposes an increase in the level of government spending can be treated in exactly the same way as an increase in private investment. We shall therefore lump private investment, I, together with spending by the government, G, and treat them as equivalent in relation to their effects on aggregate demand. The repercussions of an *increase* in the level of government spending from a level G_1 to G_2 can therefore be grasped by examining Figure 5.

By raising the level of public expenditure by the appropriate amount, the government will be able to play an active role in raising the level of effective demand, output and employment. The

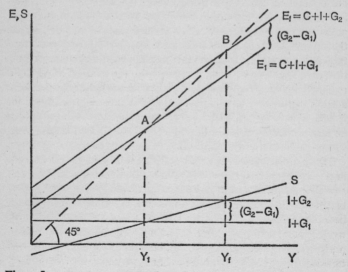

Figure 5

reader should also note that, in the position of final equilibrium, the extra spending can be funded entirely from the higher saving by the public. Inspection of the diagram reveals that saving will rise by an amount *exactly* equal to the rise in government spending. Hence the rise in the *supply* of government bonds (see Chapter 6) is precisely matched by a rise in the *demand* for bonds by the private sector.

But increases in the level of public spending are only one way of raising the level of employment. It will be recalled from our simple discussion of the components of effective demand that consumption expenditure played an important role in determining the overall level of expenditure. It therefore follows that measures which result in the stimulation of consumer spending can also play an important role in achieving full employment. Such policies are successful to the extent that they shift the consumption function *upwards* (cf. Figure 4). This can be achieved through a reduction in the general level of taxes so that firms and households have a higher level of *disposable* income (i.e. income *net* of taxes) to spend on consumer goods. The rationale behind such a policy of tax cuts is that individuals decide on how much of their income they are going to consume, by looking not at their pre-tax income, but at their post-tax income. After all, the latter is what they receive in their pay packets and is more likely to influence consumer expenditure than the former. Since tax cuts raise the level of disposable real income for a given level of gross real income, the effect of such actions will be to alter the position of the consumption function in such a way that, for each level of real income, consumption will be higher. (In Figure 3, the dotted line C′ could be the new consumption function after the tax cuts.)

Through Keynesian eyes, therefore, fiscal policy is the most important channel through which the economy can be kept on the straight and narrow path of full employment. The market cannot be relied upon to perform this function as classical economists believed. Either the market mechanism does not work at all, or it works much too slowly to be of any practical assistance to policy makers. Direct intervention through the judicious combination of taxation and public-expenditure changes is the surest method of preventing a relapse into unacceptably high levels of unemployment. In other words, fiscal policy has come to be regarded, by Keynesians at least, as the most potent ingredient of the more general policy of *demand management*, i.e. the manipulation of aggregate expenditure by the authorities in order to achieve a given policy objective (e.g. full employment) or set of objectives. That fiscal policy constitutes only one instrument in an overall strategy for demand management will become clear in Chapter 6.

Effective Demand, Fiscal Policy and Inflation

The outbreak of war in 1939 led to a dramatic fall in the unemployment rate. Indeed so pronounced was the increase in employment that the problem of unemployment, which had preoccupied economists during the inter-war period, was supplanted by the age-old problem of wartime inflation.

As we have seen, the connection between inflation and the waging of war had long been acknowledged as an unfortunate fact of life. Indeed the damaging effects of the First World War inflation were still fresh in the minds of economists and the general public alike. It was with a view to avoiding the social, political and economic vicissitudes of inflation that Keynes wrote his famous pamphlet *How to Pay for the War*.

In this pamphlet Keynes showed how the versatile principle of effective demand could be adapted to explain not only the problem of unemployment but also the phenomenon of inflation. If unemployment grew out of a deficiency of aggregate demand, then its mirror image, inflation, could be traced to an excess of aggregate expenditure over producible real income. In this case the equilibrium level of real income exceeded its full employment level Y_f: economic agents (including the government) were attempting to spend more than the economy was capable of producing. In other words the rise in government spending on armaments and other forms of war expenditure would stimulate aggregate demand to such an extent that an *inflationary gap* would be opened up. The inflationary gap is presented graphically in Figure 6.

If the economy starts off with some unemployment at a level of income Y_1, expansions in the level of government spending indicated by the upward displacement of the expenditure function will initially result in a beneficial reduction in the unemployment rate. On the other hand, once all of the unemployed have been absorbed into the productive labour force, further increases in government spending will impose excessive strain on the productive potential of the economy. Should the rise in government spending be so great as to shift the expenditure function to a position E_2, then the various claims on the output of the economy by consumers, investors and the government itself could only be satisfied if the actual output of the economy were Y_2. The problem is that Y_2, in the short term at least, is an unattainable level of output. The productive capacity of the economy is such that only Y_f units of output can be produced. There is therefore an excess demand for the output of the economy and it is this excess demand which is the root cause of this particular inflation.

Inflation can only be brought under control through a sustained policy of *demand restriction*. In terms of Figure 6, aggregate demand will have to be managed in such a way as to shift the expenditure function from E_2 to a position E_f. The inflationary gap AB is defined as the vertical distance between E_2 and E_f. Moreover if one accepts the Keynesian view that fiscal policy is the most important ingredient in an overall strategy of demand

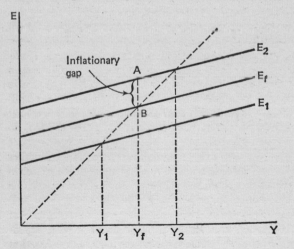

Figure 6

management then the appropriate remedy for inflation consists of raising the general level of taxation and/or reducing the level of government expenditure.

We shall return to a more detailed examination of the Keynesian view of inflation in Chapters 7 and 8. For the moment it should be noted that, although many Keynesians – especially American Keynesians – would accept that the *sources* of inflationary pressure are to be found in repeated attempts by economic agents to spend more (either now or at some time in the past) than the system is capable of producing, it does not follow that Keynesians place *exclusive* reliance upon a policy of demand restriction as a weapon against inflation. Most (?) Keynesians, and certainly Keynes himself,[2] would recommend a policy of prices and incomes restraint as a necessary adjunct to a restrictive demand policy. The enormous difficulties involved in devising an overall strategy to control inflation without at the same time plunging the economy into the abyss of an unfathomable depression require the marshalling of *all* of the instruments which policy makers have to hand. To the extent that prices and incomes policies assist in side-stepping the miseries of the mass unemployment and under-utilization of capacity that a policy which relies exclusively on demand restriction entails, then they will have performed a useful, if unspectacular service. But more of this later.

Effective Demand and the Balance of Trade

Many readers will have become a little uneasy with the assumption which we have made up to this point that the economy we are dealing with is a *closed* economy, i.e. it has no trading or financial links with the outside world. This was made necessary in order to side-step the problems which arise when the balance of payments is brought into the picture. We shall now relax this assumption and consider the implications for output and employment when the economy is *open*.

Clearly some economies are more open than others. The United States, for example, is virtually a closed economy, the flow of international trade constituting only a small proportion of its total

2. For an account of Keynes's eventual conversion to a policy of incomes control, see Trevithick (1975).

output. The US is more or less self-sufficient in the production of the goods and services which its population wishes to consume and invest. In contrast, Britain, West Germany, France, all the remaining countries of the western trading bloc and Japan are open economies, highly vulnerable to changes in the climate of international trade. For these countries, the repercussions of particular actions (e.g. increases in government spending) upon the balance of payments must be continually borne in mind when these actions are being contemplated by policy makers.

Although we shall have much to say on the problems of achieving balance of payments equilibrium later in the book, for the moment we shall simply consider what the implications of being an open economy are for the level of effective demand, and hence for output and employment. Moreover the analysis will be confined to the *balance of trade*, viz. the difference between the flow of exports of goods and services and the flow of imports of goods and services. In other words we are ignoring international *capital* movements (see Chapter 8, page 124ff.), concentrating instead on the relative movements of goods and services. The basic theme of the preceding part of this chapter was that the level of output of the economy would be determined by the amount that individuals wished to spend on the output of that economy. Clearly, in a closed economy individuals have no option but to spend their incomes on the output of their own economy. But what happens when individuals are free to spend their incomes, not only on the output of their own economy, but also on the output of another economy? What happens, for example, if British consumers suddenly find themselves able to purchase German cars instead of being forced to buy British cars? If this is not matched by an equal desire on the part of German consumers to buy British cars, the effect of such trade liberalization will be to reduce the level of output, and hence employment, in the British car industry.

Expenditure on imported goods and services must therefore be regarded as having a depressing effect on the level of output and employment which would have been higher had the expenditure on imports been channelled into expenditure on home-produced goods. Hence the calls for import restrictions so often heard in present-day Britain. Now, as we have said, nearly all economies in the western world trade with each other. To some extent this trade is occasioned by the need to import raw materials to be used in the productive process. Other imports are more accurately described as consumer goods, e.g. French wines, German cars, etc. In general expenditure on imports *rises* as the level of national income rises.[3] In Keynesian terminology, the *marginal propensity to import*, that is, the ratio of a change in import expenditure to a given change in national income, is positive.

But countries export as well as import. Just as the desire of British consumers to purchase German cars exerts a depressing effect on output and employment in Britain, so the desire of German consumers to purchase Scotch whisky, Rolls-Royces, etc., will have the opposite effect, stimulating British output and employment.

It is generally assumed that the factor which principally determines the flow of exports from one country to another is the *exchange rate* between the two countries. For example, a devaluation of the pound sterling *vis-à-vis* the dollar will, all things being equal, sharpen the competitive edge of goods produced in Britain as compared to those produced in America. For a constant pattern of exchange rates, however, the flow of exports from one country to the rest of the world will also be constant. Thus, while expenditure on imports rises as income rises, foreign expenditure on home-produced goods, i.e. exports, is invariant with the level of income. It can therefore be treated as having a similar effect on effective demand as investment (or, for that matter, government expenditure).

From the point of view of the determination of effective demand, what matters is the *difference* between exports and imports. If exports exceed imports, demand will be higher in an open economy than in a closed economy. A trade deficit, on the other hand, exerts a depressive effect on demand. Thus the 'opening up' of our

3. On the consumption side, the positive relation between imports and income is analogous to the consumption function relation: as individuals become better off, they spend more on *all* consumer goods, not just the home-produced variety. On the investment side, an expansion in output requires an increase in the input of raw materials and (perhaps) the purchase of highly specialized machinery only produced abroad.

Keynesian economy can, if it results in a trade deficit, pose a serious threat to the government's desire to maintain full employment.

In order to rectify a trade imbalance, the government has three options in our simple Keynesian scheme: (a) to reduce output and employment by restricting aggregate demand through deflationary monetary and fiscal policies (e.g. by raising taxes and/or reducing government spending) so as to reduce the flow of imports (remember that imports fall if output and demand fall); (b) to devalue the currency, thereby making exports more competitive on world markets and discouraging expenditure on foreign goods – in short, devaluations are supposed to stimulate exports and reduce imports; (c) to take steps to reduce imports directly by imposing import controls (e.g. tariffs or physical quotas) so that a *given* flow of imports can be combined with *higher* levels of output and employment. The selection of option (a) implies the abandonment of the objective of full employment in favour of the objective of trade balance, and hence is rarely considered. Option (b), devaluation, is the traditional remedy for a deficit in the balance of trade, having the added advantage that full employment need not be sacrificed. Traditional remedies, however, are not always correct. In recent years a strong body of opinion has emerged which views devaluations as being less than useful in restoring payments equilibrium. Hence the growing support for option (c). In part the disillusion with devaluations stems from the magnitude of a currency devaluation that would be required to restore the balance of payments to a more healthy state; in part it stems from the belief that the rise in domestic prices which the devaluation necessarily entails, at least in the short run, would trigger off a vicious wage–price spiral which would gnaw away a large part of the competitive advantage that the devaluation conferred on domestic producers (see Chapter 7). This school of thought tends to subscribe to one or other version of the cost-push theories of inflation and their arguments will be discussed in Chapter 7.

Keynes and the Labour Market

Trade Unions and the Sources of Unemployment in Classical Economics

In the light of the extraordinary levels of unemployment which prevailed in the 1920s and 1930s, it became progressively more difficult, as we have seen, for classical economists to extol the virtues of the self-righting properties of their system. The equilibrating mechanisms which they had assumed would work patently failed to materialize.

But how could the breakdown of the market mechanisms be rationalized? More precisely, what factors were at work preventing the real wage rate from falling to its market-clearing level? Gradually, orthodox economists of the period were forced, as we have seen, into the position of blaming the downward rigidity of the real wage rate upon the tremendously increased power of the trade union movement. Trade unions, as monopoly suppliers of labour, were able to stifle all attempts at cutting *money* wages and hence, it was argued, real wages. Either through ignorance or just pure selfishness, they were not prepared to allow wages to drift down to a position where the supply of labour equalled the demand.

Keynes's Retention of Marginal Productivity Theory

Keynes's attitude towards the classical theory of employment was partly sympathetic but mainly dismissive. On the one hand Keynes accepted the classical view that the *demand* for labour function would be determined by the shape of the marginal product of labour curve.[4] Profit-maximizing employers would indeed take on labour up to that point where the marginal physical product of labour was brought into equality with the real wage rate. The corollary of this view is that high unemployment is *associated with* an *excessively high* real wage rate.[5] To this extent, Keynes, unlike many Keynesians, had his feet firmly planted in classical ground.

4. See Chapter 2, p. 29.
5. This is the conventional interpretation of the *General Theory*. Leijonhufvud (1968) disputes this view. For a critical analysis of Keynes's theory of labour supply, see Trevithick (1976); in this paper it is shown that Keynes *did* correlate a high real wage rate with unemployment.

Keynes's endorsement of the classical theory of labour demand has profound implications which have been largely overlooked by economists who would broadly describe themselves as Keynesians. Of pivotal importance is the proposition that a decline in the real wage rate is a *sine qua non* for the attainment of full employment. Unless some means can be found for depressing the real wage rate to its market clearing level all attempts at stimulating employment will prove to be sterile.

Keynes on the Futility of Money Wage Cuts

But how are the requisite depression in the real wage rate and the consequent rise in the level of employment to be engineered? It is at this point that Keynes departs radically from the diagnosis and prescriptions of the classical economists. The orthodox view of the time was that cuts in the *money* wage would automatically be accompanied by cuts in the *real* wage. This proposition, based on the pervasive *ceteris paribus* assumption of simple price theory, assumed that employers as a whole, faced with a lower *money* price for labour, would tend to hire more of that labour. The classical remedy for unemployment therefore consisted of advising governments to implement policies involving general money wage reductions.

Keynes rejected this line of reasoning on two grounds, one empirical and the other theoretical. He first of all argued that the development of the system of collective bargaining since before the First World War rendered the downward flexibility of the money wage rate highly improbable. Attempts at cutting money wages would be fiercely resisted, as the experience of the 1926 General Strike in Britain painfully demonstrated. At first sight this may appear to be very similar to the classical proposition that trade unions are responsible for excessively high *real* wages. This is not the case. Keynes never argued that trade unions would either be willing, or, more important, be able to do *anything* about the real wage rate. The problem of unemployment was entirely out of their hands. In Keynes's own words, 'The *general* level of real wages depends on the other forces of the economic system' (*General Theory*, p. 14, original italics). What these other forces were will be discussed in a later section.

Keynes's second objection to the classical theory of employment was more fundamental. Even if trade union leaders could be induced to have a change of heart and allow the money wage rate to drift downwards, this would produce no effect on the real wage rate. A general reduction in money wages would produce an *equiproportionate* reduction in the price level. Falling money wages simply result in a situation of *balanced deflation*, the real wage rate remaining unchanged. It is for this reason that Keynes saw the trade union movement as playing a purely passive role in a plot dominated by other actors. They could neither aggravate the unemployment problem by raising money wages, nor mitigate it by accepting money wage cuts.

It is in this sense that the unemployment which bedevilled the inter-war period was classified by Keynes as *involuntary*. Unemployment of the order of 20 per cent of the available work-force could not be attributed either to the work-shyness of the population or to the bloody-mindedness of trade union leaders. Such unemployment was involuntary in that there was nothing that workers could do, either individually or collectively, to effect an overall reduction in the general level of real wages.

Demand Management and the Real Wage Rate

A central premise of Keynes's theory of employment was the view that expansions in the level of aggregate demand would exert upward pressure on the price level relative to the money wage rate whenever there existed substantial involuntary unemployment of labour. In such circumstances an increase in the level of aggregate demand will fail to put upward pressure on the money wage. To all intents and purposes, therefore, the money wage rate can be taken as a constant at less than full employment. The money wage rate only starts to creep upwards once expenditure increases push the economy towards full employment at Y_f.

The other component of the real wage rate, the price level, reacts very differently to increases in expenditure. Far from remaining constant in the face of changes in the pressure of demand, the price level is an *increasing* function of the level of expenditure even in positions of considerable under-utilization of capacity. The reason for this is that as production expanded in response to demand stimulation, the marginal cost of production would rise, putting upward pressure on the price level.

The process of real wage adjustment is illustrated in Figure 7. Clearly if, as a result of expansive fiscal policies, real income rises from Y_1 to Y_f and the price level rises from P_1 to P_2 while the money wage rate remains constant at W_1, then the real wage rate will fall to $w_f \left(= \frac{W_1}{P_2} \right)$. Full employment in the sense of the classical economists (cf. Figure 1, page 30) will have been achieved, not by 'market' forces such as money wage cuts, but by the deliberate manipulations in the scale of aggregate demand by the government. The major onus of labour-market equilibration must be borne, not by money wage cuts, but by variations in the general price level induced by prior changes in expenditure. The manner in which employment changes are umbilically linked to prior variations in expenditure by means of variations in the real wage rate is an integral part of the *General Theory*.

But was Keynes *right* in retaining the marginal productivity principle? Many of his followers regard this aspect of the *General Theory* as one of the pieces of classical luggage that Keynes had not by then unpacked. Certainly Keynes had severe doubts about the marginal productivity theory of the demand for labour *after* the publication of his great work. Indeed much of the modern work on the abstract theory of employment (see, for example, Malinvaud, 1977) indicates that, if an economy is suffering from Keynesian unemployment, a cut in the real wage rate will serve to *aggravate* the problem of unemployment by reducing the spending power of the working class. The corollary of this claim is that steps should be taken to raise the real wage rate in order to cure Keynesian unemployment. In other words, the marginal productivity principle loses all of its operational significance when there is general demand-deficient unemployment.

Keynes on the Source of Money Wage Rigidity

We have noted above that the remedy of classical economics for the problems of unemployment, viz. money wage cuts, was riddled with flaws of both a practical and a theoretical character. Even if

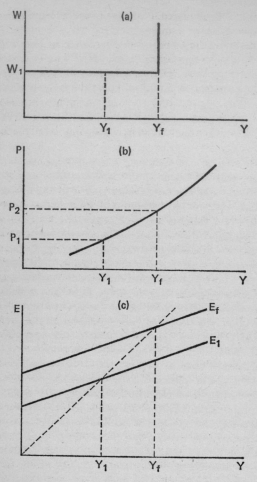

Figure 7

they did occur they would not reduce the real wage rate and hence could not form the basis for a sound policy to combat unemployment. But Keynes thought that reductions in money wages would not occur in any case. The reasons he proposed to explain the phenomenon of money wage rigidity during the 1930s can, with a little modification, be extended to encompass the case in which *wage inflation* is occurring and can be used, as we shall see in a later chapter, to provide an important justification for the implementation of prices and incomes policies in an attempt to reduce the rate of inflation.

When discussing the failure of money wages to fall in times of quite massive unemployment, Keynes regarded such downward inflexibility as being the product of a highly rigid structure of *wage differentials*. Wage bargaining was (and still is) a decentralized process in which a decision by one particular group to accept a cut in its money wage rate will probably not be followed by similar money wage cuts by other groups. Wage cuts are therefore resisted even in the face of considerable unemployment. Workers are apprehensive lest their position in the pecking order of wage differentials be damaged by following what, in simple classical theory, appears to be a rational course of action. Keynes insisted that, in practice, the operation of collective bargaining sets great store by the preservation of a highly stable pattern of wage differentials. The interconnection between different labour markets is so pronounced that any attempt at altering the structure of differentials will be strongly resisted by the groups whose relative position is threatened. Workers will go to great lengths 'to protect their *relative* real wage' and will resist any move which will disturb this relative wage. It is a well-known fact of the industrial-relations experience of most western economies that wage claims based upon comparability with other groups constitute a large proportion of all wage claims and that, if these claims are successful, they will generate a highly stable pattern of differentials over time.

Since the leaders of individual labour groups are continually looking over their shoulders at the behaviour of other groups, a spontaneous reduction in the level of money wages will fail to materialize. Moreover the same argument may be applied to a situation where the general level of money wages is rising over time. A strong dose of unemployment, which many monetarists are recommending as a cure for the current inflation, may be quite ineffective in reducing the pace of money wage increase since such a retardation requires a set of individual decisions by different labour groups, all of whom are uncertain whether other groups will follow their example in accepting reductions in the *rate of change* of their money wages. It will be shown later that the view that the *rate of money wage increase* may be subject to considerable downward inflexibility for similar reasons to those outlined above in the case of the *level* of money wages plays a significant part in the formulation of a 'Keynesian' approach to the current inflation.

Chapter 4
The Rise and Fall of the Phillips Curve

As long ago as 1926 Irving Fisher, the Yale economist of quantity-theory fame, observed a significant statistical association between the rate of inflation and the level of unemployment. He noted that in times of prosperity when aggregate spending was high and unemployment was low, a faster than normal rate of inflation tended to occur. Similarly in times of depression and high unemployment, the pressure upon prices was correspondingly reduced. Inflation and unemployment seemed, therefore, to be *inversely* correlated.

The implications of Fisher's observations went largely unnoticed by the economics profession until 1958 when Professor A.W. Phillips published a famous article on the relationship between wage inflation and unemployment. Despite Fisher's earlier research into the same area, the empirical relationships between these two variables came to be known as the *Phillips curve*.

The Phillips Curve

Phillips's Findings

Taking the results at face value, Phillips's research had unearthed quite an extraordinary inverse correlation between the rate of *wage* inflation, $\dot{W}$ for short, and the unemployment rate, U. Not only did the results appear to be impressive on purely statistical grounds, they appeared to hold good over remarkably long periods of time. Indeed for the United Kingdom there appeared to be a stable relationship between $\dot{W}$ and U for a time-span as long as ninety years.

The general nature of Phillips's relation is depicted in Figure 8.

57

The rate of wage inflation is measured on the vertical axis and the unemployment rate (the proportion of the total labour force unemployed) on the horizontal.

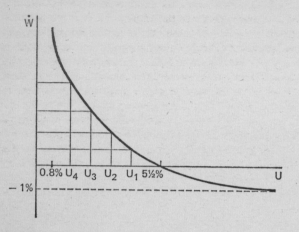

Figure 8. The Phillips Curve

For our purposes, two characteristics of the Phillips curve should be noted. The first is that the curve is non-linear. That is, successive reductions in the unemployment rate result in ever higher increases in the rate of wage inflation. For example, a reduction in the unemployment rate from U_3 to U_4 will involve a much larger increase in the rate of wage inflation than would an *equal* reduction in the unemployment rate from U_1 to U_2. Indeed the relationship predicted that as U approached 0·8 per cent, wage inflation would approach infinity. The second characteristic is that, once the curve passes below the horizontal axis, it becomes perceptibly flatter. This has often been regarded as an empirical vindication of Keynes's view that even at high rates of unemployment, money wages would not fall to any appreciable extent. The *minimum* rate of wage inflation predicted by the Phillips curve was of the order of minus one per cent.

In Chapter 3 we encountered a theory, the theory of the inflationary gap, in search of empirical ballast. In this chapter we have come across a statistical association, the Phillips curve, in search of a theory. A marriage is clearly in the offing.

From the point of view of empirical testing, the inflationary-gap theory has a number of shortcomings, the most serious of which is the difficulty of devising an adequate measure or yardstick by which to gauge how near to full employment we actually are. More specifically we require some measurable indicator of how near to *full-capacity* working the economy is operating. Since the inflationary gap theory postulates that inflation occurs when Y exceeds Y_f, and since we are in practice unable to measure the discrepancy between Y and Y_f, attempts at testing this theory are likely to founder unless an indicator of the size of the inflationary gap can be constructed.

The principal contribution of Phillips's study lay in his suggestion that a reasonably reliable indicator of capacity utilization[1] may be found in the unemployment rate. According to this line of reasoning, an increase in the level of capacity utilization, produced, for example, by expansive fiscal policies, will be mirrored in a reduction in the unemployment rate. Fluctuations in the unemployment rate can therefore be regarded as observable manifestations of changes in the underlying pressure of aggregate demand.

One final hypothesis is required before the Phillips curve can be taken as the empirical counterpart of the theory of the inflationary gap. This is the hypothesis that the *rate* of wage (and price) inflation will depend upon the *magnitude* of the inflationary gap. The larger the vertical distance AB (see Figure 6, page 45), the larger will be the ratio $\dfrac{Y}{Y_f}$ and the *faster* will be the pace of wage inflation. In the terminology of Chapter 3, we would expect the rate of inflation to be higher whenever there are forces at work (e.g.

1. There are various ways, in principle, of measuring the degree of capacity utilization. We can either take the *difference* $(Y-Y_f)$ or the *ratio* $\dfrac{Y}{Y_f}$.

consumer booms, new public-expenditure projects) which tend to shift the total-expenditure function upwards.

The Phillips Curve as a Menu for Policy Choice

In the late 1950s and for most of the 1960s, a veritable army of researchers sprang up, all of whom devoted their very considerable technical expertise to refining and elaborating Phillips's basic hypothesis. More variables were included, more sophisticated econometric techniques were applied and alternative measures of the degree of capacity utilization were tried out. However nothing new in principle was added to Phillips's basic contribution.

Moreover it was not long before economists and policy makers alike began to grasp the wide-ranging implications of a stable Phillips curve. If an inverse relation existed between the rate of inflation and the level of unemployment, could not the authorities manage demand in such a way as to be able to strike a balance between an 'acceptable' unemployment rate on the one hand and a similarly 'acceptable' rate of inflation on the other? Could not a positive rate of inflation be regarded as the price which had to be paid for a policy of full employment? Gradually economists came to look upon the Phillips curve as a *trade-off* relation in the sense that each time policy makers were tempted to reduce the unemployment rate by a certain amount, rationality demanded that they compare, in their minds' eye at least, the benefits arising from the lower unemployment rate to the detrimental effects of a higher rate of inflation. The Phillips curve was a constraint which all realistic policy makers had to acknowledge and incorporate into their strategy for managing aggregate demand. It is in this sense that the Phillips curve was regarded as a menu for policy choice: for a given structure of the labour market and for given 'external' factors such as the rate of change of import prices, the authorities could only choose those combinations of inflation and unemployment which lay *along* the Phillips curve. To hanker after a zero rate of inflation and a 2 per cent unemployment rate was an attitude of irresponsible self-delusion.

It should also be noted that, although the Phillips curve gave considerable support to the theory of the inflationary gap, there is nothing inherently Keynesian in the notion of a trade-off between inflation and unemployment. Indeed many of Keynes's followers, particularly in Britain, regarded the Phillips curve with deep suspicion. This group of Keynesians put much greater emphasis upon certain institutional factors affecting the labour market to explain the upward movement of money wages (see Chapter 7). They regarded the Phillips curve as a statistical freak, a *trompe-l'œil*: its ultimate breakdown after 1967 appeared to vindicate this attitude of deep suspicion. In brief, the collapse of the Phillips curve can in no way be taken as evidence, as some monetarists have claimed, of the futility of Keynesian demand management.

Friedman's Theoretical Repudiation of the Phillips Curve

All seemed to be going well for the Phillips-curve industry right down to 1967 when Milton Friedman's presidential address to the American Economic Association was delivered. This was an event of singular importance in the development of the theory of economic policy, marking as it did a return to a much older, pre-Keynesian tradition in its analysis of the twin problems of inflation and unemployment. Friedman denied that the Phillips curve was anything other than a purely transitory phenomenon. In the medium-to-long period, policy makers did not in fact enjoy any discretion over which inflation–unemployment policy to pursue as economists of the previous decade had believed. There is *no* long-term trade-off between inflation and unemployment.

According to Friedman, Phillips's error consisted of confusing the *money* wage rate with the *real* wage rate. (The reader will recall that this is precisely the criticism which Keynes levelled at the classical economists, but that is another story.) Instead of measuring the rate of change of the money wage rate on the vertical axis, Phillips should have measured the rate of change of the money wage rate *minus* the anticipated rate of change of prices. To demonstrate how Friedman arrived at this conclusion, it is necessary to prepare the ground by reconsidering a few basic propositions of pre-Keynesian economic theory.[2]

2. Henceforward referred to as *neo*-classical theory. Keynes's use of the term 'classical' tended to be somewhat indiscriminate, lumping together economists as diverse as, for example, Adam Smith and Alfred Marshall.

Real Wages and the Natural Unemployment Rate

Pre-Keynesian economists tended to analyse the labour market, as they would any other market, in terms of the classic pressures of supply and demand. An excess supply of labour would result in downward pressure on the real wage rate through the operation of market forces. Similarly excess demand for labour would have the opposite effect, raising the real wage rate and ultimately establishing full employment.

It is customary to assume that the greater the excess demand for labour, the faster the rate of increase in the wage rate. But whereas Phillips concentrated upon the dynamics of adjustment of the *money* wage rate, the proper object of attention should, according to orthodox theory, be adjustments in the *real* wage rate. Since both the demand for and supply of labour varied with the real wage rate, employment variations could only be accomplished through variations in the real wage rate, at least in the long run. For example, in Figure 1 (page 30), the real wage rate will fall more rapidly if the initial real wage rate is w_2 than if it is w_1. Gradually, as the real wage rate falls towards w_e, its rate of decrease will fall towards zero since at w_e the supply and demand for labour will be equal.

Neither Friedman nor Keynes would assert that there will be *no* unemployment once full employment has been reached at the market clearing real wage rate w_e. Even in the most tightly stretched economy there will always be *some* unemployment associated with structural rigidities in the labour market and with the frictional unemployment produced by workers changing jobs and registering as unemployed while looking for another job. The existence of structural and frictional unemployment implies that measured unemployment will never be zero.[3] Bearing this in mind, therefore, Friedman has proposed the concept of the *natural unemployment rate* which, in its most innocent guise, is that unemployment rate consistent with supply/demand equilibrium in the

3. Indeed for most of his active career Keynes doubted whether the unemployment rate in Britain could be brought permanently below 5 per cent of the working population. By post-war standards this appears to be a remarkably high figure.

labour market. The natural unemployment rate is that proportion of the labour force which will remain unemployed[4] even though the overall supply of labour has been brought into line with the demand for labour through equilibrating variations in the real wage rate. In other words the unemployment rate corresponding to the *employment* rate L_f will be the natural rate.

Here we may observe the recrudescence of the pre-Keynesian view that market forces, operating through the real wage rate, will automatically guarantee full employment at the natural unemployment rate. We have seen how Keynes retained – wrongly perhaps – the classical view that a fall in the real wage rate was a necessary condition for a rise in employment. What he totally rejected was the notion that automatic forces would spontaneously produce the necessary variations in that rate. If the invisible hand of free enterprise could have been relied upon to restore full employment equilibrium in the labour market, then the *General Theory* need never have been written.

The Natural Unemployment Rate and Inflationary Expectations

A more conventional way of approaching Friedman's natural-rate hypothesis is to examine the reaction of economic agents to an *actual* rate of inflation over and above the rate that they *expected* to occur. For illustrative simplicity let us assume that there is no productivity growth, so that changes in wages will be exactly matched by equiproportionate changes in prices; and that wages and prices are expected to be stable into the indefinite future. In such circumstances, the actual and expected rates of wage and price inflation will be zero. Moreover if we assume for the moment that the Phillips curve is an accurate representation of economic reality, it follows that the only unemployment rate where the assumption of wage/price stability actually holds true is where the Phillips curve crosses the horizontal axis. This, according to Friedman, is an alternative way of looking at the natural unemployment rate – that it is the only rate at which *actual* and *expected* rates of inflation are equal.

In order to clarify this proposition and also to see why a trade-off between inflation and unemployment cannot persist in the long

4. Clearly the *same* people need not be unemployed year in year out.

run, let us draw a standard Phillips curve which cuts the U-axis at a 5 per cent unemployment rate (see Figure 9 below). Since our hypothetical economy is assumed to have enjoyed a long period of wage/price stability which is expected to continue into the future, we deduce that the economy *must have been* operating at a pressure of aggregate demand consistent with a 5 per cent unemployment rate. But let us now assume that policy makers have swallowed whole the Phillips-curve literature and have decided to trade off, say, a 3 per cent unemployment rate against, say, a 6 per cent rate of inflation. The authorities now believe that a 6 per cent rate of inflation is the price worth paying for a 3 per cent unemployment rate.

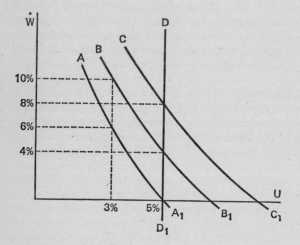

Figure 9

For the first time in its recent history, our hypothetical economy has started to experience positive inflation. Initially, according to Friedman, all will be well and the government will be content with their successful reduction in the unemployment rate. The crucial question is: If the government remains committed to the indefinite maintenance of a 3 per cent unemployment rate, will the price of such a policy *remain* 6 per cent inflation? Friedman's answer to

64

this is unequivocally negative. The price will mount cumulatively since there will be a continual tendency for inflation to *accelerate* over time.

Consider Figure 9 once again. The rise in the rate of wage and price inflation to 6 per cent initially coaxes more workers on to the labour market in the false belief that their *real* incomes are also increasing at 6 per cent per annum. Employers will want to take on more labour, since they initially pay more attention to the increase in their revenues than to the increase in their costs. Gradually, however, both groups will come to realize that they have been confusing money quantities with real quantities. The newly attracted workers will eventually realize that their real wages have not been rising at all and will withdraw their labour. Similarly employers will realize that the real cost of hiring labour has not fallen at all and will cut back on their demand for labour. The reactions of workers and employers reinforce each other and, if left unimpeded, the economy will return to the natural unemployment rate.

The mechanism by which the unemployment rate returns to its natural value is illustrated in Figure 10, which is adapted from Friedman (1975). Once again L^s, L^d and w represent the supply of labour, the demand for labour and the real wage rate respectively. Starting

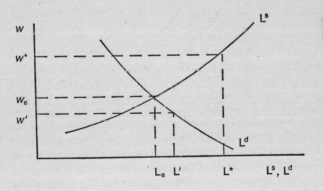

Figure 10

off in a position of full equilibrium at the natural employment rate, L_e, let us assume that aggregate money demand is stimulated by expansionary monetary and fiscal policies. A level of employment in *excess* of L_e can only be realized to the extent that employers and workers are confused into making the *opposite* mistakes concerning the behaviour of the real wage rate. More specifically, employers must think that the real wage rate has fallen and thus be induced to demand more labour, while workers must think that the real wage rate has risen and thus be induced to supply more labour (it is conceivable, though unlikely, that the *actual* real wage rate will remain unchanged during the process of adjustment). Let the real wage rate perceived by the employers be w' and the real wage rate perceived by workers be w^*. The supply of labour rises to L^* while the demand for labour rises to L'. The actual employment rate is determined at the short end of the market, i.e. by the smaller of L^s and L^d. From the way in which Figure 10 has been drawn, L^d ($=L'$) is smaller than L^s ($=L^*$) so that the actual level of employment is L'. Nonetheless, with the passage of time, both employers and workers will come to realize that they have misread the market signals. Once this happens employers will no longer be willing to hire extra labour and workers will no longer be willing to provide extra man-hours: both the demand for and supply of labour will fall to L_e (provided, of course, that the real wage rate is at w_e). Moreover, if workers and employers do *not* misread market signals in this way, the unemployment rate can never fall below the natural rate. 'Only surprises matter' (Friedman, 1977, p. 12): the government can only cause changes in the level of output and employment, say the monetarists, by catching the private sector, and particularly workers and employers, off their guard. If the government does not succeed in confusing the private sector then the ability of demand management policies to alter real variables is non-existent.

If the authorities *do* succeed in catching the private sector 'on the hop' and hence in depressing the unemployment rate below its natural value, an important development will take place in the period of adjustment back to full equilibrium at L_e. It takes time for the self-righting processes within the labour market to work themselves out. Government-induced inflation could last for a sufficiently long period of time for *inflationary expectations* to be generated. In this case the economy would indeed ultimately return to 5 per cent unemployment but the build-up of inflationary expectations by both workers and employers during the period of transition permanently alters the nature of the new equilibrium.

For example, let us assume that at the end of the period of transition from a 3 per cent back to a 5 per cent unemployment rate, the expected rate of inflation has risen from 0 to 4 per cent. Since equilibrium in the labour market is defined with respect to the *anticipated real wage rate*, that is the real wage rate that workers estimate they will be able to command and employers estimate they will have to pay, an expected rate of change of wages and prices of 4 per cent will be perpetuated in the new equilibrium. Since the expected real wage rate is the ratio of the expected money wage rate to the expected price level, the belief on the part of employers and workers that prices and wages will continue to rise at 4 per cent will in no way be affected by the return of the unemployment rate to 5 per cent. The actual and expected real wage rate will eventually converge upon w_e, with both the numerator, W, and the denominator, P, rising at 4 per cent per annum.

The most striking feature of the monetarist theory of employment is the manner in which it has returned to pre-Keynesian methods of analysis. Just compare Figure 10 with Figure 1 and a remarkable similarity will be observed. Deeply embedded in monetarist theory is the supposition that, in a market economy, full employment will automatically be established through variations in the real wage rate and that deviations from full employment are caused by erroneous calculation or expectation by employers and workers. In the opinion of this author, the jettisoning by the monetarists of the principle of effective demand in favour of a glamourized version of classical employment theory is a highly retrogressive step.

Short- and Long-Run Trade-Off Relations

According to the argument of the last section, there is no long-run trade-off between inflation and unemployment. The government may *attempt* to achieve an unemployment rate of 3 per cent, but the underlying forces of supply and demand will, after some period of adjustment, pull the unemployment rate back to its initial level of 5 per cent. During the process of adjustment, however, inflationary expectations will build up so as to make inflation a permanent feature of economic life. The 5 per cent unemployment becomes associated, not with a zero rate of inflation as the Phillips curve would appear to indicate, but with a 4 per cent rate of inflation.

Let us now assume that the government disapproves of the return of the unemployment rate to 5 per cent and, despite the presence of a 4 per cent rate of inflation, decides to embark on another spending spree in order to bring the unemployment rate back to 3 per cent. Once again, they will *temporarily* succeed in achieving their unemployment objective, but since the expected rate of inflation is now 4 per cent, this success can only be bought at the price of a 10 per cent rate of inflation (6 per cent + 4 per cent). And once again market forces will tend to bring the unemployment rate back to 5 per cent, but this time the adjustment period will raise the expected rate of inflation to 8 per cent (Figure 9). In this case wages and prices will be rising at a rate of 8 per cent per annum even though the unemployment rate has returned to 5 per cent. It is clear from the above example that over-ambitious employment policies will drive a wedge between actual and expected rates of inflation. Individuals, having failed to anticipate inflation correctly in the first place, will attempt to rectify their error by revising their expectations of inflation upwards. Nevertheless in so doing they merely increase the *actual* rate of inflation still further.

Each time the government tries to depress the unemployment rate below its natural rate, the rise in the actual rate of inflation will eventually come to be anticipated by workers, employers and all other economic agents involved in nominal contracts extending into the future. In other words each time the demand management authorities attempt to defy the realities of the market place and achieve 'over-full' employment, there will be a continual tendency for the Phillips curve to drift in a 'north-easterly' direction. A given Phillips curve therefore cannot be regarded as a stable relation whose existence into the foreseeable future can be guaranteed. It is purely a short-term phenomenon. Indeed there will be an infinite set of short-term Phillips curves, each one corresponding to a different expected rate of inflation.

Three such curves are illustrated in Figure 9. The AA_1 curve corresponds to a zero expected rate of inflation; the BB_1 curve to a 4 per cent rate; and the CC_1 curve to an 8 per cent rate. In the long run the only unemployment rate which is consistent with a *stable* rate of inflation is the natural rate. At all other unemployment rates, inflation will either accelerate or decelerate. It is therefore clear that the natural unemployment rate is consistent with *any* rate of inflation, depending on the precise position of the relevant short-term Phillips curve. In our example, the natural rate of unemployment is consistent with a zero, a 4 per cent or an 8 per cent rate of inflation. Inflation is the result of present or past attempts of the authorities to maintain unemployment below its natural rate. In the long run the only choice which the authorities face is which point along the vertical line DD_1 they are eventually prepared to settle upon.

The Rational Expectations Hypothesis

When we discussed the formation of inflationary expectations in the preceding sections of this chapter (p. 63ff.) it was assumed the expected rate of inflation would change only as a result of prior changes in the *experienced* rate of inflation. Stated more formally, individuals were supposed to predict the future behaviour of the price level by extrapolating from past changes in the price level or in the rate of inflation (see p. 71 below). In recent years a more radical group of monetarists has emerged whom we shall call the *rational expectations* school. This school asked the question: why should rational agents, in forming their expectations of future price movements, confine their attention solely to information provided by a time series of the price level or of changes in the price level? Why should they not harness other information, and, in particular, information concerning 'the economic structure', in order to predict the future course of the price level? As we have already seen, the earlier monetarist literature assumed that economic agents initially confused real with nominal magnitudes but that, in time, this confusion would be sorted out and employment would readjust to its full employment level. The rational expectations school took this approach one step further, arguing that, as the economy becomes accustomed to the experience of inflation, economic agents become very adept at distinguishing relative price changes from changes in the absolute price level. Furthermore – and this is the really controversial aspect of their approach – rational economic agents will have an incentive to formulate for themselves the 'correct theory' of what determines changes in the price level. Though this school admits the *possibility* of other theories being correct, they almost invariably restrict their detailed analysis to the monetarist theory of inflation. Despite the intense controversy which rages among professional economists concerning the sources of inflationary pressures, it is claimed that the ordinary trade unionist, the ordinary employer, even the ordinary housewife, are all in a position to discern 'the correct theory': naturally they decide in favour of monetarism. The public has eventually to realize through bitter experience of past inflation that money is neutral, i.e. that it does not affect real variables, and this realization itself *makes* money neutral even in the short run. In contrast to the earlier monetarist literature where changes in the money supply affected the price level via the level of aggregate real demand, the rational expectations school now argues that such changes alter the price level directly: real variables such as employment, output and the real wage rate remain unchanged. This consideration has recently led a critic of Keynesianism to remark: 'The rational expectations philosophy represents a devastating critique of the rationale for Keynesian-type budgetary policy which makes no allowance for the fact that the private sector will anticipate the behaviour of the government itself' (Chrystal, 1979).

The corollary of this hypothesis is that inflation can be reduced much more painlessly than earlier monetarists had thought. Provided that the government can convince the public that it intends to keep the money supply under strict control, the absolute price level will respond with only a very short lag. Thus widely publicized money supply targets announced for long periods of time can, it is claimed, go a long way in reducing the rate of inflation. Moreover, since money is neutral in the short run as well as the long run, the extent of the underutilization of resources which a normal 'demand restriction' policy entails will be minimal. One of the strongest objections to the monetarist cure for inflation – that it would require substantial unemployment, a wastage of plant, enterprise and expertise, a reduction in private capital formation, etc. – is claimed to have been answered.

Empirical Evidence

Empirical Tests of the Natural-Rate Hypothesis

In fact a large number of econometric studies for the United States and Britain tend to confirm the common-sense view that the expected rate of inflation – *in addition to* the unemployment rate – is a powerful determinant of the actual rate of inflation. These studies provide an important vindication of Friedman's assertion that the expected rate of inflation at any point in time is the legacy of past attempts by well-intentioned but short-sighted governments to maintain unemployment at unrealistically low levels. The methodology of the empirical tests of Friedman's model, though highly complex in detail, is fairly simple to grasp in principle.

For a given expected rate of inflation, the actual rate of inflation will indeed vary with the unemployment rate as Phillips predicted. Friedman's analysis differs from Phillips's in that, in the longer period, Friedman asserts that the expected rate of inflation ($\dot{P}^e$) will itself depend upon the unemployment rate. In particular, if the government aims at an unemployment rate such that the actual rate of inflation ($\dot{P}$) exceeds the expected rate, the expected rate of inflation will itself tend to rise, since individuals will attempt to rectify their under-anticipation of inflation. In other words, so long as $\dot{P}$ exceeds $\dot{P}^e$, $\dot{P}^e$ will be rising. This should be clear from the previous example. The only situation in which $\dot{P}^e$ will be neither rising nor falling is when $\dot{P}^e$ is equal to $\dot{P}$, i.e. where the unemployment rate is at its natural rate.

The controversial aspects of these studies lie in the manner in which inflationary expectations are estimated. This is a technical matter of some complexity which we shall steer clear of. In general it is assumed that the expected rate of inflation is some sort of weighted average of past rates of inflation. Once a time series for $\dot{P}^e$ has been generated, the actual rate of inflation, $\dot{P}$, is then correlated with both the unemployment rate and the expected rate of inflation, i.e. equations of the form $\dot{P} = f(U) + \dot{P}^e$ are estimated by standard techniques. These equations are known as *expectations-augmented* Phillips curves since they take explicit account of the importance of expectations in conditioning the overall inflationary climate.

The Empirical Breakdown of the Phillips Curve

Much to Friedman's credit, his attack on the Phillips curve, and the scope for government discretion in demand-management policies which it implied, was launched when the Phillips curve was still very much a going concern. Friedman's rejection of the Phillips curve took place against a background of continuing confidence in the concept as a predictive relationship. It may not have had much justification in terms of traditional economic theory, but it did at least appear to exist. After around 1968, however, certain rather disturbing developments started to cast doubts upon the Phillips curve as a relationship capable of reliable prediction. After that date rising unemployment rates were associated with *accelerating* rates of inflation in many western countries, most strikingly in the United Kingdom. How could such phenomena be explained? Clearly they stand in stark contradiction not only to the basic prediction of the simple Phillips curve which would associate rising unemployment rates with a slow-down in the pace of inflation but also to the 'stable natural unemployment rate' hypothesis.

Several rival hypotheses have been advanced to explain the simultaneous occurrence of rising inflation and rising unemployment. Although we shall not consider them in detail at this stage, three important explanations can be listed: (1) unemployment rising to its natural rate; (2) changes in the natural unemployment rate itself; (3) the positively-sloped Phillips curve; (4) cost-push factors. For the moment we shall concentrate on explanations (1) to (3), postponing consideration of explanation (4) to a later chapter.

(1) From the above explanation of Friedman's rejection of the Phillips curve, it is evidently possible for both the unemployment rate and the rate of inflation to rise simultaneously provided that the unemployment rate is rising from a level *below* the natural rate. If, for example, U is rising from 3 per cent towards 5 per cent, we

have seen that the expected rate of inflation will also rise during this period of transition. Moreover, to the extent that the expected rate of inflation exerts an important influence over the actual rate of inflation, Friedman's analysis suggests that rising unemployment rates and rates of inflation will coexist for as long as unemployment is rising towards its natural rate.

(2) A second explanation for the breakdown of the Phillips curve lays greater emphasis on the notion that the natural unemployment rate may itself be increasing over time as a result of changing conditions in the labour market. If, for example, the distribution of unemployment between various regions, occupations or industries is becoming more uneven, a given overall pressure of demand may correspond to a higher unemployment rate. In more technical language, increases in the structural and frictional components of the unemployment rate may have distorted the accuracy of the *total* unemployment rate as an indicator of the pressure of aggregate demand. There is some evidence that, at least for the United Kingdom, the unemployment rate is becoming progressively less reliable as a proxy variable for the degree of capacity utilization, conflicting as it does with other commonly used indicators.

A further monetarist explanation for the rise in the natural unemployment rate is that it reflects an increase in *voluntary* unemployment: the rise in unemployment benefits as a proportion of the real wage rate has induced many workers to opt for unemployment. Thus Friedman (1976) wrote: 'In Britain and the United States we have made unemployment a very attractive situation. In my country many a person can have as high an income in real terms by being unemployed as he can by being employed. The laws of economics work very well: if there is a demand for anything, the supply will tend to rise to meet the demand. If there is a demand for unemployed people, then the supply of unemployed people will rise to meet it.'

But once the notion of a *stable* natural unemployment rate is so drastically modified by the *force majeure* of recent economic history, the monetarist theory of employment and inflation starts to border on the tautological. Originally a rising rate of inflation was taken by the monetarists as evidence that the unemployment rate *must have been* below the (given) natural rate. The experience of recent years has been characterized by rising inflation and by unemployment rates which are enormously high by the standards of the post-war period. Only explanation: the natural unemployment rate must *also* have been rising. In the absence of corroborative research into the response of labour supply to, for example, changing unemployment benefits, this 'explanation' should be demoted to the rank of 'unsubstantiated conjecture'.

(3) While Professor Friedman accepts the view that the natural unemployment rate has been rising owing to 'excessively generous' unemployment benefits, he has gone a good deal further than many of his followers in acknowledging the awkward facts of economic life thrown up by the experience of the 1970s. In his Nobel Lecture (Friedman, 1977) he frankly recognized that the stable natural-rate hypothesis did not fit the facts. But Friedman was undaunted by this observation: he put forward the theory of the temporary, but *positively*-sloped, Phillips curve. Inflation, he claimed, *caused* unemployment by interfering with market signals concerning actual and expected relative prices. The consequent disruption of the market mechanism would therefore cause unemployment to be higher than it would otherwise have been. However, Friedman argued that once inflation came to be fully anticipated the Phillips curve would once again become vertical and the unemployment rate would return to its natural rate. The only snag is that 'such a transitional period may extend over decades'. It is surprising to observe the lengths to which monetarists will go in defending the cherished notion of the natural unemployment rate.

Chapter 5
Monetarism

The Twilight of Keynesianism

The Disillusion with Keynesian Economic Policy

The failure of successive governments in different countries to contain inflationary pressure has led to a parallel disillusionment with demand-management policies in general and with Keynesian economics in particular. Governments and their economic advisers were all too easily tempted, it is claimed, to apply with excessive enthusiasm Keynesian principles for boosting the economy. Instead of allowing market forces to establish full employment (these are, of course, monetarist critics), they fell into the false belief that they could challenge market realities and maintain politically more acceptable unemployment rates into the indefinite future. But sooner or later the facts of economic life assert themselves in the form of ever-accelerating rates of inflation. According to Friedman, governments should stop playing God, pretending that they can fashion for themselves an employment policy which is independent of the latent forces of supply and demand within the labour market.

It is a point of some contention whether Keynes would have disagreed with Friedman's rather pessimistic diagnosis. We have seen from Chapter 3 that Keynes regarded fiscal policy as an important propulsive force for the attainment of full employment. Nevertheless it should be recalled that full employment for Keynes, as for Friedman, occurs where there is overall equality between the supply of and the demand for labour. The fact that fiscal policy may play a useful role in edging the economy towards a position of labour-market clearance should not lead on to the dubious proposition that governments are in a position to *define for themselves* what is the appropriate level of unemployment to be aimed at. The use of fiscal policies in maintaining levels of employment in excess of L_e (see Figure 1, page 30) can only lead to a situation of what Keynes called 'true inflation'.

How Keynes's name came to be associated with employment policies commonly described as 'Keynesian' is a question which is best left to historians of economic thought. It is a pity that the current debate between the monetarists and the Keynesians has been marred by the citation of the crudest form of Keynesian model, a model which ignores the fact that the objective of any sound aggregate employment policy must be to strike a balance between the supply of labour on the one hand and the demand for labour on the other, taking due account of the regional and occupational dispersion of unemployment. It is even more disturbing to observe how Keynes's ideas have been interpreted in certain political circles as supporting indiscriminate expansionism and ever-widening powers of state intervention in everyday economic life. In fact Keynes loathed inflation with all the intensity of Professor Friedman. In some circumstances (e.g. wartime or an otherwise uncontrollable boom) he would have been one of the first to advocate *contractionary* policies to remove the threat of inflation.

The lines of demarcation which are supposed to discriminate between Keynesian and monetarist interpretations of the origins of inflation and unemployment are very inaccurately drawn. To a large extent this confusion can be traced to the inevitable bowdlerization of Keynes's ideas which accompanied their incorporation into elementary text-books. But surely of no less significance is the strong desire on both sides to erect straw men, not only to facilitate skilful and dramatic demolition, but also to create the background for a more clamorous public debate. Simple theories with even simpler slogans abound, and the ghosts of defunct economists have been invoked either to add lustre to otherwise commonplace opinions or to provide the focus for misdirected attack. In both respects, the subtle complexity of Keynes's theory of prices and employment has been the most conspicuous victim.

For some inexplicable reason the breakdown of the crude Phillips curve greatly undermined confidence in the Keynesian approach to economic policy and contributed to the already growing popularity of monetarism. But we have already seen how the 'stable natural unemployment rate' hypothesis – an integral part of modern monetarism – was similarly called into question by the events of the 1970s. Moreover the incorporation of the Phillips curve into an otherwise Keynesian model of the economy may have been a reasonable procedure in the 1960s when the Phillips curve did at least appear to exist, but strictly speaking it has absolutely nothing to do with Keynesianism. The gist of Keynes's writings is quite easy to grasp. Starting from the demonstration that a capitalist economy could remain in a position of substantial underemployment of resources for quite long periods of time, Keynes went on to show how active demand management, particularly through the instrument of fiscal policy but including a policy of monetary accommodation, would succeed in stimulating the economy to a position of full employment *without* inflation. The Keynesian model is not first and foremost a theory of the determinants of the price level or the rate of inflation; it is a theory of the determinants of aggregate demand in real terms and thereby a theory of output and employment. On the other hand, Keynes and his followers always recognized that if aggregate real demand exceeded full capacity output (see p. 44ff.) there would be a connection between the extent of excess demand and the rate of inflation. Nonetheless it was felt that the link between the level of aggregate demand and inflation in an *underemployed* economy was weak to the point of non-existence. The co-existence of *in*voluntary unemployment and, for example, rising inflation – a phenomenon which the monetarists almost rule out by assumption – is explained by the hypothesis that money wages and prices rise on account of certain non-competitive forces, particular attention being focused upon the interaction of powerful trade unions and equally powerful oligopolies.

Keynesianism, Fiscalism and Demand Management

For over thirty years after the publication of the *General Theory*, Keynesian methods of demand management held sway in the macroeconomic policies of most western countries. These methods were based on the belief in two propositions, one concerning the *scope* of demand-management policies, the other concerning the preferred *technique* of demand management.

77

irst was the belief that governments enjoyed a considerable
it of discretion in the employment policies adopted. The un-
earthing of the Phillips curve added an extra dimension to the
problem of demand management in that policy makers were intro-
duced to the dilemma of having to trade off a lower unemployment
rate against a higher rate of inflation. Nevertheless governments
still retained considerable room for manoeuvre in determining
whether to follow an expansive or a contractionary demand-
management policy. What they now had to bear in mind were the
inflationary consequences of different employment policies as
made explicit in the Phillips curve (a relation rejected from the
very beginning by many Keynesians).

The second assumption underlying Keynesian attitudes towards
demand management was the view that fiscal policy was the most
potent weapon for controlling the level of aggregate demand. By
varying the relationship between its expenditure and its revenues,
the government would be able to generate quite large changes in
aggregate demand. To the extent that it exerted a powerful influence over the level of aggregate spending, fiscal policy could thereby induce major changes in output, employment and (perhaps) the
rate of inflation. By implication, other techniques of demand
management, most notably variations in the supply of money,
were regarded as being secondary in importance. Indeed many
Keynesians, suffering from an excess of zeal for fiscal policy, were
occasionally heard to utter the view that changes in the money
supply had *no* effect on the level of aggregate demand. In the minds
of many of Keynes's followers, Keynesianism came to be identified
with *fiscalism*.

The Revival of Monetarism

Professor Friedman, the high-priest of monetarism, mounted a
three-pronged attack on these well-entrenched canons of Keynesian orthodoxy. Stated simply, his objections to Keynesianism
are: (a) that the government does not enjoy the elbow room in
implementing its own employment policy that the simple Phillips
curve appears to imply; (b) that the most important determinant

78

of aggregate spending is the supply of money; (c) that for a *constant rate of increase* in the supply of money, unemployment will eventually settle down at its natural rate and the rate of inflation will ultimately be equal to the difference between the rate of increase in the supply of money and the rate of growth of output.

We have already dealt with the first proposition in Chapter 4 when we discussed Friedman's dismissal of the simple Phillips curve. In that chapter it was assumed that the government, if it so wished, would have the means at its disposal to maintain unemployment at a level below the natural rate, at least in the short run. We left unanswered the obvious question of *how* the government would be able to depress unemployment below its natural rate, albeit temporarily.

The Supply of Money and Aggregate Demand

According to Friedman, the only means by which the government will be able to maintain unemployment below the natural unemployment rate for considerable periods of time is through a policy of ever-accelerating monetary expansion. Underlying Friedman's position is the view that, far from being the minor supernumerary of Keynesian theory, *monetary policy* exerts the most powerful influence over aggregate spending. Increases in the supply of money (or, more accurately for modern economies, increases in the *rate of increase* of the supply of money) generate much more pronounced increases in aggregate demand than do equivalent increases in the size of the budget deficit. This relegation of fiscal policy to a relatively minor position and the reinstatement of monetary policy as the principal technique of demand management is the hall-mark of monetarism.[1]

In Friedman's treatment of the labour market there is, as we have already observed, a striking similarity between Friedman's views and those of pre-Keynesian economists. Market forces, operating through the price mechanism, will frustrate attempts by the government to achieve artificially low unemployment rates. Moreover if the government can be persuaded to abandon its

1. Of course the rational expectations wing of monetarism (see Chapter 4) does not accept even this proposition, since it regards demand management by whatever means as a pretty futile exercise.

futile attempts to boost aggregate spending and raise employment, these same market forces will eventually push unemployment towards its natural rate. It should come as no surprise, therefore, that Friedman should have been the principal architect of the reconstruction of the quantity theory of money, though in the opinion of the present author, Friedman has added little to the analysis of inflationary processes that was not already present in the works of quantity theorists such as Fisher and Pigou.[2]

Starting off from a position of full employment (i.e. a position where unemployment is at its natural rate) and a position of price stability, a once and for all increase in the supply of money will temporarily stimulate expenditure on goods and services as individuals attempt to offload excessive money balances. That is, unemployment will temporarily fall below its natural rate. Moreover the excess demand occasioned by the increase in the money supply[3] will tend to raise the price level until the demand for money once again equals the supply of money. Once this position of monetary equilibrium has been restored, the excess demand will have vanished and unemployment will have risen back to its natural rate.[4]

But suppose that we have a stubborn government bent on defying the realities of the market-place and determined to maintain unemployment below the natural rate (for example, an unemployment rate of 3 per cent in Figure 9). How can it achieve this objective? Friedman's answer is: Only by maintaining persistent excess demand which, in turn, requires the *continual* issue of new money. We have seen above that a once and for all issue of new money will *initially* manifest itself in the form of an excess demand

2. Friedman has made many central contributions to the general area of monetary theory. The contention here is that in his diagnosis of the monetary sources of inflation, his analysis, especially in his more recent writings, is not appreciably different from older quantity theorists' views. For a more positive view of Friedman's contribution to this area, see Laidler and Parkin (1975).

3. Precisely *how* the government increases the supply of money is a question of great importance, the discussion of which is postponed to Chapter 6.

4. We are assuming here that inflationary expectations are not generated to any appreciable extent as a result of the once and for all rise in the price level.

for goods and services, but that the beneficial repercussions on employment of such an isolated action will soon be dissipated in higher prices. Repeated injections of new money are therefore necessary if this policy of 'overfull' employment is to be successful.

Monetary Expansion and the Natural Unemployment Rate

If the maintenance of, say, a 3 per cent unemployment rate requires successive injections of money by the monetary authorities, the quantity theory of money predicts that the price level will rise continually over time. The picture might not be too bleak if this were the end of the story, but it is not. According to the analysis of Chapter 4, continually rising prices will eventually become incorporated into individual expectations regarding the future course of the price level. Inflation, if experienced for a long enough period of time, will come to be anticipated in all money contracts, including the wage bargain struck between employers and workers. We saw how a demand-management policy which aimed at a 3 per cent unemployment rate could only be paid for at the price of an accelerating rate of inflation. The corollary of this proposition is that such an unemployment rate can only be maintained by continually increasing the *rate of increase* in the supply of money, i.e. by issuing new money at an ever-increasing rate. If carried to its logical extreme, the monetarist view predicts that the attempt to peg the unemployment rate at 3 per cent will ultimately involve the decline into hyper-inflation and a total collapse of the currency.

Suppose now that the government perceives the danger signals in time and decides to exert some degree of control over the supply of money. More specifically let us assume that the government attempts to *stabilize the rate of monetary expansion*, i.e. to allow the supply of money to grow at a *constant* proportional rate. In terms of the present analysis, such a policy implies that the government is abandoning its role as initiator of variations in aggregate demand, being no longer willing to exert an independent influence over aggregate spending. Just as in the simplest case where *no* increase in the supply of money will, according to monetarists, produce a situation of price *stability*, a constant rate of monetary expansion will lead to a constant rate of inflation.[5] Moreover,

5. More accurately, the rate of monetary expansion, $\dot{M}$, will equal the rate of inflation, $\dot{P}$, plus the rate of growth of output, $\dot{Y}$, i.e. $\dot{M} = \dot{P} + \dot{Y}$.

once the government recognizes the error of its ways and stops interfering with the market mechanism, unemployment will eventually return to its natural rate.

The Monetarist Cure for Inflation

The essence of the monetarist remedy for inflation should be obvious by now. Since inflation is the result of past and present attempts by governments to over-utilize the productive capacity of the economy through the issue of new money, inflation can only be reduced by cutting the rate of monetary expansion. The objective of price stability can only be achieved by allowing the supply of money to grow at a rate equal to the rate of growth of real income.[6] Nor will a policy of monetary restraint be without its painful side-effects for it implies a considerable period of *under-utilization* of capacity and high unemployment. Inflation can only be successfully tackled by reversing the direction of the policies which produced the inflation in the first place. A régime of strict monetary restraint will therefore be accompanied by unemployment rates in excess of the natural rate, for it is only thus that the necessary erosion of inflationary expectations can occur. If the government is determined to conquer inflation, it must be prepared to stomach the unpopular consequences implicit in a policy of monetary contraction.[7] An inflationary binge will inevitably be followed by a deflationary hangover.

But monetarists do not stop at recommending a policy of strict control over the supply of money. They also proceed to condemn all other methods of reducing the rate of inflation, most notably prices and incomes policies. They assert that monetary control is the *only* policy which will make an appreciable impact on the rate of inflation. Not only do prices and incomes policies fail to have any lasting effect on the rate of inflation, they can be positively harmful in that they involve widespread interference by the government in the process of wage and price determination. Since

6. This prescription has to be amended when there are clear signs of long-term changes in the velocity of circulation of money.

7. In this context a policy of monetary contraction is one where the rate of monetary expansion is being reduced. It is not one of absolute reduction in the size of the money stock, merely a reduction in its rate of increase.

monetarists also tend to set great store by the virtues of market forces and resent most forms of direct government intervention, it is natural that they should reject a policy of prices and incomes control, representing as it does an unwelcome suspension of the price mechanism. Monetarists reject the view that prices and incomes policies are an effective way of side-stepping the unpleasant withdrawal symptoms which they regard as the ineluctable by-product of a programme of demand restriction. The best thing to do with a hangover, they say, is to endure it.

The rational expectations wing of the monetarist school also agrees that prices and incomes policies will not permanently reduce the rate of inflation but will simply distort the allocation of resources and produce greater inefficiency all round. However they do not see the 'hangover' problem as being at all serious. Since the private sector is in possession of the 'correct' model of how the economy works (the 'correct' model being, of course, the monetarist model), all the government has to do is announce money supply targets for some years to come, convince the public that it intends to stick to those targets and then carry out what it has announced. If this policy of persuading the omniscient public that the government means business succeeds, quite a substantial reduction in the rate of monetary expansion can be effected with minimal extra unemployment and lost output. The mechanism of eroding inflationary expectations by deliberately under-utilizing capacity – the more traditional monetarist cure for inflation – will have been short-circuited, or so it is claimed.

Keynesian Rumblings

One of the cornerstones of the monetarist theories of inflation is the claim that a strong association exists between rising prices and increases in the stock of money. What many Keynesians object to is the interpretation in monetarist terms of what is merely a statistical association. Many Keynesians – for example, Kaldor (1970), Robinson (1971) – argue that prices rise for reasons other than the excess demand produced by prior monetary expansion. They maintain that, in economies where the government is pledged to a policy of full employment, the trade union movement may take advantage of this commitment and press for ever higher wage increases. In the absence of monetary expansion, such wage increases will raise the unemployment rate over time, or at least to that point where unemployment is so high as to impose some degree of restraint on wage demands. Nevertheless, in the light of the full employment commitment of most governments since the Second World War, sustained trade union pressure for higher wages will *produce* expansions in the supply of money.

Keynesians emphasize that by far the larger component of the money supply is made up of bank deposits and that changes in the volume of bank deposits closely reflect changes in the volume of lending by banks. Hence if a bank extends a loan to an individual or firm and a cheque (say) is issued on the strength of this loan in order to meet some financial commitment, the lodging of the cheque in the account of the recipient individual or firm will serve to raise the volume of bank deposits and thereby raise the money supply. For example, let us assume that a firm decides to spend more: this could be the result of an increased desire to hold larger stocks of components and raw materials; it could be the result of a desire to take on more labour as a result of an actual or expected rise in the demand for the firm's product; or it could be the result of irresistible pressure from trade unions for higher wages. Inso far as the extra outlay is financed either by the taking up of unused overdraft facilities or by a new loan arrangement, the act of expenditure will automatically raise the money supply since the deposits of the recipients of the extra spending (the raw materials and components suppliers, etc.) will rise *pari passu*. Another example of how the money supply will rise automatically in response to an exogenous increase in expenditure is when the government wishes to raise public spending while at the same time preventing a potentially damaging rise in the rate of interest. If this extra public spending is not financed out of higher taxes it must be financed either by borrowing from the public through the sale of bonds or by borrowing from the banking system (see Chapter 6). If the authorities take the first course of action – that of financing the whole of the rise in the budget deficit by selling bonds to the public – there will be a distinct danger of the rate of interest rising. In general, governments wish to prevent disruptive fluctuations in the rate of interest so they are often induced to finance *part* of the deficit by borrowing from the banking system (which includes the Central Bank), at least in the short run.[8] But the effect of such a method of finance is very similar to the effect of extra borrowing from banks by firms or individuals: the total volume of bank deposits rises and, as a result of the convention of defining the money supply in such a way as to include bank deposits, the money supply rises.

In both of these cases – the case of an autonomous rise in business or household spending and of an autonomous rise in government spending – the increase in the supply of money was the result of prior increases in *ex ante* expenditure which, once realized, necessarily raises the volume of bank deposits.[9]

The implications of this interpretation of the statistical evidence are far-reaching. Far from indicating that an increase in the stock of money was the prime mover in an inflationary process, the evidence should be read the other way round. Increases in the price level *call forth* accommodating increases in the supply of money. Stated more formally, the supply of money is itself a function of the price level, and the rate of monetary expansion is therefore a function of the rate of inflation. The price level (or the rate of inflation) is the independent variable, at least in a narrowly economic model of inflation.

Nor do Keynesians stop here in their criticisms of the monetarist interpretation of inflation. They regard the monetarist analysis of the labour market as naive; the downgrading of fiscal policy as unwarranted; the relationship between monetary and fiscal policy as inadequately explored; and the lumping together of diverse sources of monetary expansion as gravely misleading. These are serious charges which will be examined in greater detail in the following chapters.

8. In the Keynesian system a budget deficit can always find its ultimate funding in the rise in saving that occurs as a result of the rise in income (see Figures 3 and 5). However, at the higher level of income the rate of interest will, in general, be higher unless steps are taken to raise the supply of money. For this reason budget deficits will be *initially* financed by a mixture of bond finance and monetary finance (see Chapter 6, p. 96ff.)

9. We are ignoring for simplicity the case where there is a substantial volume of 'idle' money balances which can, in principle, be activated to facilitate a rise in spending.

Chapter 6
Monetary Versus Fiscal Policy

The traditional issue which separates Keynesians from both old and new monetarists has revolved around the relative importance to be attributed to fiscal policy on the one hand and to monetary policy on the other in the determination of the overall pressure of demand. Keynesians have persistently argued that fiscal policy is by far the most powerful instrument which the authorities have at their disposal for manipulating the pressure of demand, the level of employment and (perhaps) the rate of inflation. Monetarists, quite naturally, adopt a contrary view, asserting that aggregate demand can most effectively be regulated through variations in the size or rate of change of the money stock.

One of the objectives of this chapter will be to show that many of the apparent areas of conflict between Keynesians and monetarists on this issue can be traced to a confusion on both sides as to the precise meaning of the terms *fiscal* policy and *monetary* policy. According to monetarists, monetary policy is the set of instruments which the authorities have at their disposal to control the *supply of money*. Thus an expansionary monetary policy is one which entails an increase in the rate of monetary expansion. Similarly, when implementing a contractionary monetary policy, the authorities should, by definition, aim at reducing the rate of monetary expansion. We shall see later on in this chapter how Keynesians take a rather narrower view of monetary policy, concentrating particularly upon the *interest-rate* effect of varying the supply of money. Thus whereas a monetarist, when trying to evaluate the stance of monetary policy, would tend to look at the behaviour of the money supply, a Keynesian would tend to look at the behaviour of the rate of interest.

Fiscal policy poses no problem of definition. Fiscal policy is the deliberate manipulation of the relation between government expenditure and government receipts with a view to manoeuvring the level of aggregate demand in the desired direction. By increasing the size of the budget deficit, the government hopes to stimulate the level of output and employment, possibly at the price of a higher rate of inflation. Restrictive fiscal policies, involving a reduction in the budget deficit, are intended to produce the opposite effect of reduced output and employment and also of a lower rate of inflation. We have seen above how Keynesianism has unfortunately come to be identified with fiscalism in the sense that fiscal policy has been regarded, in Keynesian circles, as the most powerful instrument for controlling the level of aggregate demand.

The origins of this terminological confusion can be traced to the practice, widespread among both monetarists and Keynesians, of treating monetary and fiscal policy as independent instruments. This is, in fact, far from being the case. For example, an increase in the budget deficit can generate a considerable increase in the rate of monetary expansion if it is financed by borrowing from the banking system instead of the sale of bonds to the public. The corollary is that one very important method of reducing the rate of monetary expansion consists in reducing the budget deficit. Past failure to acknowledge the high degree of interdependence between monetary and fiscal policy is largely responsible for the unnecessary confusion of the 'monetary *versus* fiscal policy' debate.

The Monetarist View

The simplest and most extreme monetarist view is that fiscal policy is a very weak instrument of demand management. This is not to say that monetarists do not regard government expenditure, taxation and the budget deficit as unimportant. On the contrary, such variables are of critical relevance in two principal respects. Firstly, the size of the public sector has immediate implications for the allocation of resources. Monetarists generally argue that the private sector knows better how to allocate resources than the government. This, of course, is not a question of how the government controls the pressure of demand. Rather it is a question of how resources should be distributed between competing uses, public and private. Secondly, and more relevant for our present purposes, the size of the budget deficit has direct implications for monetary policy, for the excess of government expenditure over taxation receipts has to be financed in some way, and this will necessarily have implications either for the supply of money or the general level of interest rates or both. In the event of the budget deficit being financed by the issue of new money, then this will be expansionary. The importance of the budget deficit is, therefore, that it constitutes one potential source of monetary expansion. There are, however, other possible sources of increase in the money supply, and if we limit ourselves to the simple case of a closed economy, then the most important of these is open-market operations, of which we have much to say below.

Once the money supply is increased, from whatever source, monetarists believe this will have a direct impact on money income, via the cash-balance transmission mechanism outlined in Chapter 2. Individuals who 'find themselves' holding excessive money balances spend the excess on goods and services. If the economy started off in a position of full employment, prices would rise. On the other hand, if the initial position was one of substantial unemployment and under-utilization of capacity, the principal effect of such expenditure would take the form of higher output and employment. In contrast to the indirect Keynesian mechanism outlined later, monetarists prefer to regard changes in the money stock as *directly* affecting expenditure on goods and services.[1] Increases in the money stock do not have to depend upon the complicated chain of reaction which is an integral part of the Keynesian view of monetary policy. In general monetarists adroitly duck the inevitably complex question of how the increase in the supply of money is engineered in the first place, lumping together all forms of monetary expansion and treating them as equivalent in their impact on demand, at least in the long run. Indeed in one celebrated essay, Professor Friedman (1969) side-stepped the complexities, which a complete analysis of the different channels

1. For an illuminating, though depressingly propagandist statement of the difference of opinion between monetarists and Keynesians, see A.A. Walters, *Money in Boom and Slump*, Institute of Economic Affairs, Hobart Paper no. 44, pp. 18–19.

through which the money supply can increase would entail, by assuming that the money supply rose as a result of the scattering of dollar bills from a helicopter. This example of how an increase in the supply of money might take place is instructive, not because monetarists actually believe the money supply is altered through this mechanism, but because it illustrates the relative unimportance which monetarists attach to distinctions between different sources of monetary expansion. (Some of the more recent monetarist literature has recognized this point but it has yet to make much impact on vulgar monetarism.)

The Keynesian View

Monetarists thus regard manipulation of the money supply as the most important technique of demand management. In contrast Keynesians emphasize the pre-eminent role of fiscal policy as a technique of demand management. Why do Keynesians laud the virtues of fiscal policy, by implication downgrading monetary policy? What *is* the Keynesian view of monetary policy?

When Keynesians refer to monetary policy at all, they have in mind a technique of control known as *open-market operations*. It is *this* form of economic management which has fomented so much disagreement between the monetarists and those Keynesians who bother to give any consideration to monetary policy. Open-market operations, normally undertaken on behalf of the government by the central bank, affect two important variables – the supply of money and the rate of interest.

The general public hold government bonds so as to take advantage of the fact that, like other financial assets, they pay interest and may, if bought at the right time, yield a capital gain. The advantages of holding an interest-bearing asset (e.g. a government bond or a share in General Motors) over holding an asset which bears no interest (e.g. money) should be fairly obvious. Open-market operations rely for their efficacy upon the fact that the general public will be willing to surrender part of their holding of bonds to the central bank if the bank is willing to offer a sufficiently attractive (i.e. high) price for those bonds; and will be willing to acquire government bonds if the bank offers them for sale at a sufficiently low price. Open-market operations are the sale or purchase of government bonds on the open market by the central bank.

But *how* do open-market operations influence the supply of money and the rate of interest? Let us take the example of open-market purchases of government bonds by the central bank from the general public (the same principles apply, *mutatis mutandis*, to open-market sales). As was indicated above, the bank must be prepared to offer to buy bonds from the public at a sufficiently high price in order to induce the public to part with bonds, which earn interest, in exchange for money, which earns no interest. The fact that the higher prices being paid for bonds will be exactly mirrored in a fall in the rate of interest will be dealt with in the following paragraph. For the moment it should be noted that the surrender of bonds by the public is matched by an equivalent increase in the supply of cash in the hands of the public. The public voluntarily sells £x million worth of bonds *in exchange for* an equivalent amount of cash. The reduction in the public's holding of bonds is exactly matched by an equal increase in their holding of cash. Moreover in a *fractional reserve system* in which the overall supply of money is some fixed multiple of the supply of cash in circulation, open-market purchases will lead to a multiple expansion in the supply of money.[2]

But open-market purchases do not only lead to increases in the money supply. They also lead to *reductions* in the interest rate. Let us assume, for example, that before the central bank had decided to engage in open-market purchases, the market price of government bonds was £1,000 and that the annual fixed payment on each bond was £100 payable in perpetuity. In this case the interest rate on government bonds was 10 per cent. In order to engage successfully

2. The supply of money is normally defined as notes and coin in circulation *plus* the volume of bank deposits. The inclusion of bank deposits is made necessary by the fact that, in sophisticated financial systems such as those of the UK and the US, the majority of transactions are effected, not by the exchange of cash, but through the exchange of cheques drawn on bank accounts and other forms of 'book-keeping' devices. The relationship between the supply of cash and the overall supply of money, though easy to grasp in principle, requires more detailed examination than is possible in this book. The reader who would like to pursue this topic further should consult R.G. Lipsey, *An Introduction to Positive Economics*, Weidenfeld and Nicolson, 4th ed., Chapter 42.

in open-market purchases, however, the bank will have to offer a price in excess of £1,000 for each bond in order to induce the public to surrender the appropriate amount of interest-bearing bonds in exchange for cash. Suppose the bank finds it so difficult to separate the public from its bonds that it is forced to offer a price of £2,000 per bond. That is, the market price of bonds will double, while the annual money return from each bond (£100) remains unchanged. The percentage yield on bonds has therefore fallen from 10 per cent to 5 per cent. The investor who wishes to move into government bonds will only be able to command a percentage return of 5 per cent on his investment. In other words, the market rate of interest on bonds has fallen to 5 per cent.

Nor is this the end of the story. Since government bonds are fairly close substitutes for other sorts of financial asset such as stocks and shares in private companies, the upward pressure upon the price of bonds will be accompanied by similar rises in the prices of private-sector securities. In other words the fall in the rate of interest payable on government bonds will be paralleled by a *general* decline in interest rates.

Given these effects, the question which Keynes asked was: How can such open-market purchases possibly boost the level of aggregate demand? Was a policy which, by definition, merely reshuffled the total composition of the wealth of the economy away from bonds and in favour of money really to be regarded as expansionary in the sense that it increased aggregate spending?

In Keynes's opinion, the principal channel through which an open-market purchase could stimulate demand and employment lay in its impact on the general level of interest rates. By reducing the rate of interest, open-market purchases would lead to an increase in the flow of investment which would, in turn, lead to a multiple expansion in demand through the multiplier mechanism. The lower the cost of capital, as represented by the rate of interest, the greater would be the incentive for entrepreneurs to invest and the higher would be the level of national income. Keynes therefore saw monetary policy, which he identified with open-market operations, working as follows: increases in the supply of money are associated with reductions in interest rates; lower interest rates induce entrepreneurs to invest more; and the higher flow of investment leads to a multiple expansion in aggregate demand; this in turn will lead either to higher real income or higher prices, depending upon whether the economy started off in a position of under-employment or full employment.

In this schema there are two vital links both of which must hold good if open-market purchases are to exert a significant influence on the pressure of demand. Firstly, the rate of interest must fall as a result of such a policy. Secondly, in the face of the fall in interest rates entrepreneurs must make a substantial upward revision in their investment plans. In other words, the rate of investment must be fairly sensitive to variations in the rate of interest. Although Keynes had the prudence to steer well clear of making dogmatic pronouncements on such basically empirical questions, some Keynesians have not shared their master's caution. They have asserted (a) that the rate of interest may not be appreciably reduced by open-market purchases, and/or (b) that even if the interest rate *does* fall as a result of such policies, the rate of investment will not rise since the decision to invest is dominated by considerations other than the cost of capital. In these theories, the impact of monetary policy (i.e. open-market operations) is negligible.

It should be noted that this analysis of the effects of monetary policy is based on the notion that individuals hold larger money balances as a result of a *voluntary* decision to swap (at the right price, of course) bonds for money. In no sense can individuals be regarded as *finding themselves* holding excessive money balances. It is at this point that the terminological confusion regarding the *source* of increases in the supply of money becomes clearly perceptible. As was pointed out previously, Keynesians deliberately confine discussion of monetary policy to open-market operations. Indeed, without doing too much injustice to the Keynesian camp, for monetary policy one can substitute *interest-rate policy*: monetary policy is not principally concerned with controlling the supply of money as such but with controlling the rate of interest, for it is only through this channel that it can ultimately affect demand.

It has often been argued by eclectics that, though the Keynesian indirect mechanism may be more appropriate in describing the reaction of the economy to increases in the money stock produced by open-market purchases, the cash-balance mechanism, much favoured by monetarists, may be more accurate when the increase in the supply of money occurs through the scattering of bank notes over large towns from helicopters. The first reaction of these fortunate inhabitants to finding the streets paved with £5 notes is likely to be to spend their (literally) windfall gains.

Not even the most die-hard Keynesian would deny the validity of the cash-balance mechanism in the case of helicopter money. What Keynesians baulk at is the tendency among monetarists to treat helicopter money as being identical in its effect on aggregate demand to open-market operation money.[3] Does the mere re-distribution of a given stock of money wealth between money and bonds, implicit in open-market operations, really have just the same impact on demand as a *net addition* to this stock through the dispersal of newly printed money from helicopters? Keynesians rightly claim that the former sources of monetary expansion have much weaker effects on aggregate demand than the latter (patently unrealistic) source.

The Keynesian View of Fiscal Policy and its Monetary Implications

According to the highly stylized formulation of the Keynesian system presented in Chapter 3, aggregate demand consists of three components: consumption, investment and government spending. Whereas fiscal policy can be used to regulate all three components of demand, monetary policy can only affect the level of investment (and even then by a highly circuitous route). By raising the level of its own expenditure or by lowering the general level of taxes the government will exert a powerful influence over the level of aggregate spending. In other words, variations in the size of the budget deficit will produce sympathetic variations in the level of demand. Moreover if private investment stubbornly refuses to revive and overall consumption patterns remain largely un-changed, the simple Keynesian model predicts that the government

3. For a more detailed attack on the monetarists for their *simpliste* aggregation of the various sources of monetary expansion, see Lord Kahn, *On Re-reading Keynes*, Proceedings of the British Academy, Vol. LX (1974), p. 9 ff.

may have to run a budget deficit indefinitely (see Figure 4, page 39). But the sceptic may ask: How does the government *finance* this permanent deficit?

Deficit Finance, Crowding Out and the Supply of Money

Expressed crudely, the government has only two financial options open to it if it wants to run a larger budget deficit. It must either borrow more from the public, or it must issue new money by borrowing from the banking system.

It is the assumption of most Keynesian models that the government will opt for the first course of action, i.e. deficit borrowing. Since the supply of borrowable funds (i.e. savings) rises with the level of national income (remember that the marginal propensity to save is positive), the government will be able to harness this extra saving in the form of higher borrowing from the public once the level of national income has risen as a result of the operation of the multiplier process. As full employment is approached, however, it will prove to be progressively more difficult to finance higher budget deficits from funds borrowed from the public. Indeed once full employment has been reached, the flow of savings will have reached an *absolute maximum*. Thenceforward further increases in the government's budget deficit can only be achieved at the expense of private investment.

For example, assume that the full employment level of savings is £6,000m., that the level of government spending is £2,000m. and that the level of private investment is £4,000m. In this case, private savings are just sufficient to satisfy the expenditure plans both of the government and of private investors. On the other hand should the government attempt to raise its own expenditure to, say, £3,000m., such a policy can only be successful to the extent that it reduces private investment.[4] Stated differently, the rise in the public-sector deficit at full employment has the effect of 'crowding out' private investment so that the *net* effect on aggregate demand

4. In a more complete analysis allowance would have to be made for the fact that part of the rise in government spending could come from a fall in consumption as well as from a fall in investment. Nevertheless the ultimate result is the same – demand remains more or less unchanged. This complication is ignored in what follows.

is negligible. The stimulating effect of a higher level of government spending financed by borrowing is exactly offset by the contractionary effects of a lower level of private investment.

The same result does *not* hold good when the government resorts to less orthodox methods of financing a higher budget deficit. If, instead of borrowing from the general public, the government decides to issue new money to finance its more ambitious expenditure plans, then the impact of such a policy upon aggregate demand will be strongly expansionary. For example, if the government decides to build an expensive motorway but is unwilling, for whatever reason, to finance this project either out of higher taxes or from borrowing, it can borrow from the central bank in order to pay for the motorway. Such a form of monetary expansion is probably the closest a modern economy will ever come to the scattering of bank notes from helicopters,[5] for the money enters *directly* into circulation in payment for the goods and services involved in building the motorway. Instead of aggregate spending being the *last* variable to be affected, as in the case of an open-market purchase, an increase in the supply of money, produced by a rise in government spending not matched either by higher taxes or by borrowing, will *first of all* be experienced in the form of increased purchases of goods and services.

Crowding Out at Less than Full Employment

We have seen how, at full employment, financing a budget deficit by borrowing from the public will have no net effect on aggregate spending. This result was derived from the sound Keynesian view that the supply of savings at full employment was fixed (or could only be raised at the expense of consumption expenditure).

In recent years, however, a school of thought has grown up (or, more accurately, re-emerged) which states that the same conclu-

5. The parallel between monetary expansion through budget deficits and helicopter money is not strictly accurate. Whereas it is just conceivable (though extremely unlikely) that the lucky recipients of helicopter money will not spend their windfall gain, budget deficit money, by definition, *is* expenditure, in this case on the part of the government. How much of this extra expenditure is in turn spent by its recipients depends upon the size of the marginal propensity to consume.

sion holds true even when the economy is in a position of *less* than full employment. According to this group of monetarists, crowding out can occur in the presence of substantial under-utilization of capacity, rendering powerless a policy of fiscal intervention. This is a revival of what, in Britain, used to be known as the *Treasury view*, which stated that a rise in government spending could only be achieved to the extent that it deprived private investors[6] of an equivalent supply of finance.

This view can be expressed in simple Keynesian terms in the following way. The flow of savings (that is, the supply of finance for investment) depends principally upon the level of income. Before an increased flow of savings can be generated, therefore, the level of income must *already* have risen to a new higher level. But how is the initial increase in income which is supposed to generate the higher flow of savings to be itself generated? According to the monetarists, the most effective way of stimulating spending and hence national income is by increasing the stock of money (or the rate of monetary expansion). Variations in M exert a much more powerful influence upon national income than do variations in the difference between government expenditure and government receipts (G–T).

Keynes, Crowding Out and the Role of Monetary Expansion

Although Keynes's *General Theory* gave rise to a whole new way of looking at economic policy, it has very little to say on the more detailed aspects of policy. Nevertheless much of the subsequent debate between Keynes and his critics revolved around the practical implications of expansive fiscal policies, especially measures to increase public expenditure (the 'loan expenditure' referred to by Keynes). In this debate Keynes was to make several important amendments to the analysis of the *General Theory*[7] which we shall briefly summarize.

6. The Treasury view was articulated in opposition to proposals for public works to alleviate the unemployment problem between the two World Wars. It came in for a considerable amount of criticism from Keynes and his Cambridge followers.

7. Many of the amendments are more accurately described as elaborations and additions. For a blow-by-blow account of the post-*General Theory*

Economic expansion produced by direct government intervention should be regarded as a two-stage process. The first stage is one of true expansion which occurs through the financing of a higher budget deficit by the issue of *new money*. By issuing new money and injecting it directly into circulation, the government will be able to finance a higher level of its own expenditure without at the same time depriving the private sector of the available supply of loanable funds for investment. Moreover the effect of a higher flow of government expenditure will be to raise the level of national income through the familiar Keynesian mechanism described in Chapter 3.

The second stage of the process is more familiar. Once the level of national income has risen to a more acceptable level as a result of the injection of extra purchasing power into the economy, the supply of loanable funds from a higher volume of savings will also increase (see Figure 5, page 42). The government will then be able to *maintain* national income at this new, higher level by borrowing from this larger volume of savings.

The Keynesian multiplier process, set in motion by a rise in (G–T), should therefore be seen as consisting of two stages:

(1) the expansionary stage where the rise in the budget deficit is financed by monetary creation;

(2) the consolidation stage where the rise in the budget deficit can be financed out of the higher volume of savings generated as a result of the initial expansionary stage.

It should be clear from this argument that attempts to demonstrate the superiority of monetary over fiscal policy, or vice versa, are ill-founded. Although monetary expansion *can* operate in the absence of sympathetic variations in the size of the budget deficit (that is, if the supply of money is increased by open-market operations), the stimulating effect of such a policy is likely to be at best very roundabout and of uncertain magnitude. By far the more direct method of varying aggregate spending is by increasing the budget deficit, financing this increase by the issue of new money. Thus *variations* in the level of aggregate demand are most effec-

debate, the reader is referred to *The Collected Writings of John Maynard Keynes*, edited by Donald Moggridge for the Royal Economic Society, Volume XIV.

tively engineered by the adoption of stage (1) of the Keynesian multiplier process outlined in the previous section. The *maintenance* of the new higher level of demand will require the implementation of stage (2) of the same process. Hence, although increases in M can stimulate demand (albeit indirectly) without any change in (G–T), for fiscal policy to be effective an increase in (G–T) will have to be implemented by means of an initial phase of monetary expansion.[8]

We are now in a position to draw a few tentative conclusions regarding the relative efficacy of monetary (open-market operations) and fiscal policies:

(a) If monetary policy is implemented independently of fiscal policy, its impact on aggregate spending will depend upon a complicated and uncertain chain of reaction.

(b) If fiscal policy is implemented independently of monetary policy, its impact on aggregate spending *might* be relatively small, though there is still considerable dispute on this point.

(c) If monetary policy and fiscal policy are treated as *complementary* policies, then their impact on aggregate spending will be considerable. Thus, for example, if an increase in the money supply is engineered *as a result of* a larger fiscal deficit, the stimulating influence on effective demand will be immediate and direct.

Conclusion

A common feature of some Keynesian and all monetarist theories of inflation is the view that a sufficiently large *reduction* in the level of aggregate expenditure will lead to a fall in the rate of inflation. If the origins of inflation can be traced to present or past attempts to run the pressure of demand at 'excessive' levels, then, by a symmetry of reasoning, inflation can be brought under control only by reversing the policies which produced the inflation in the first place. What this amounts to is the adoption of demand-management policies which will have the effect of *under-utilizing*

8. Following Keynes's later writings, we are here assuming that the volume of idle hoards of money which can be re-activated to finance government borrowing is negligible.

capacity: in Professor Friedman's terminology, of maintaining unemployment above its natural rate.

According to the above analysis, such policies will require the simultaneous implementation of restrictive monetary and fiscal policies. The rate of monetary expansion will have to be reduced (at a very gradual pace, according to the monetarists) and the most efficient method of achieving this objective is to reduce the size of the budget deficit. Once again, greater emphasis should be laid on the complementarity of monetary and fiscal policies.

Taken together, Keynes's *General Theory* and his pamphlet *How to Pay for the War* can be regarded as attempts to apply the same principles of analysis to two entirely different situations. In the *General Theory*, Keynes's principal concern was with the problem of massive and prolonged unemployment and the remedies he advocated all had the single objective of stimulating aggregate expenditure so as to achieve full employment without inflation. In *How to Pay for the War*, however, his preoccupation was with the management of an economy which was not only fully employed, but over-employed in the sense that there was an excess of effective demand over producible real income. The remedy for this latter case, the case of what Keynes called 'true inflation', consisted in adopting policies to reduce the pressure of demand. In the wake of the spectacular success of the *General Theory*, Keynes quite naturally supported policies of fiscal restriction, i.e. policies to reduce the size of the budget deficit. Latter-day monetarists, on the other hand, would place greater emphasis on the role of monetary restriction, i.e. reducing the rate of increase in the money stock. We have seen above that the monetarist and Keynesian prescriptions need not be regarded as *rival* remedies for inflation. The most effective means of implementing a restrictive monetary policy may be to reduce the size of the budget deficit. It is regrettable that the virulence of the largely semantic debate between monetarists and Keynesians has concealed the considerable amount of common ground that unites the two camps.

Although the confused debate regarding the relative impact of monetary and fiscal policies on aggregate demand has occupied the attention of economists for a number of decades, we shall see in the next chapter how the emphasis of the 'Keynesians versus neoclassicals' debate has shifted perceptibly in the last few years, especially in Britain. Instead of quibbling over the preferred method of demand management, many Keynesians[9] have asserted that restrictive demand policies, however implemented, will have very little effect in tempering the pace of inflation. These Keynesians have espoused what has come to be known as the *cost-push* approach to the problem of inflation. This approach will be the theme of the following chapter.

9. According to Lipsey (1975), p. 757n, '. . . there are probably as many strands of neo-Keynesian thought as there are Oxbridge colleges'.

Chapter 7
Cost-Push, the Labour Market and the Control of Inflation

In the previous chapters we have noted a considerable degree of consensus among some (mainly American) Keynesians and monetarists regarding the ultimate sources of inflation. Although varying degrees of emphasis were placed upon the effectiveness of monetary and fiscal policies in generating or moderating inflationary pressure, both camps agree that inflation can be traced to excessive expenditure which, in a more or less fully employed economy, bids up the price level. Persistently excessive expenditure leads not only to inflation but to *accelerating* inflation on account of the important role which inflationary expectations play in determining the experienced rate of inflation (see Chapter 4, page 63).

There is a very influential school of thought which totally rejects this line of reasoning. For want of a better label we shall refer to the rival interpretation of the sources of inflationary pressure as the *cost-push* view. At its simplest, the cost-push school regards the increases in costs of production as the principal source of inflationary pressure. For example, the recent increase in the world price of oil is often blamed for much of the current inflation. Similarly increases in the costs of imported goods resulting from a devaluation of the currency is often regarded as adding an undesirable new twist to an already acute inflationary problem.

Nevertheless, by far the most popular version of the cost-push interpretation of inflation is one which pins most of the blame on the monopolistic practices of trade unions. It is argued that, by exploiting their undoubted power as monopoly suppliers of labour, trade unions ask for and receive 'unreasonable' wage increases which in turn provoke price increases. Furthermore these price increases, by eroding the real value of the new money wage, lead to a further demand for higher wages. And so the mechanism continues, monopolistic unions bidding up the money wage and, after some lag, the price level, which in turn leads to a further demand for higher wages. The process is likened to a cat chasing its tail with ever-increasing fury.

In the following three sections we shall analyse.

(1). different versions of the cost-push approach;

(2). the difficulties which arise in discriminating between cost and demand pressures on a national basis;

(3). the formulation of a Keynesian view of the inflationary process which integrates some of the more acceptable features of cost-push and excess-demand explanations.

Cost Inflation

Simple Theories

According to standard supply/demand analysis, an excess demand for the commodity being offered on a market will tend to raise the price of that commodity. Similarly, competitive theory would predict that an excess of demand over supply in the labour market will raise the price of labour, i.e. the wage rate (see Chapter 2, page 31). Moreover, since labour is a vital element in the production process, a general increase in the wage rate will raise the price of output, i.e. the general price level. Thus although the increase in the price level may be the *immediate* result of the higher money wage rate, the *ultimate* origin of higher prices lies in the excess demand for labour (and presumably for commodities also). These are the rudiments of an excess-demand theory of inflation which have been discussed in the previous chapters. In periods of excess aggregate demand, *all* prices rise, including the price of labour. The fact that the costs of inputs into the productive process also rise during such periods in no way invalidates the view that the source of inflation was excessive expenditure, past or present.

The advocates of the cost-push interpretation reject this view as being archaic, nineteenth-century economics. We no longer live in a world of unbridled competition where market forces would ensure that overall price stability would prevail at full employment and where mild deflation would be experienced at less than full employment. On the contrary, they argue that our world is one dominated by large monopolies where powerful unions can dictate the terms of the wage bargain with impunity and where the power of large corporations to bargain on equal terms is no less. Standing on the side-lines is the government, which is always prepared to step in to maintain full employment through its monetary and fiscal policies should the power struggle between unions and employers result in such exorbitant wage increases as to endanger full employment. With the government always ready to intervene, the 'normal' outcome of such a process, higher unemployment, is not allowed to emerge. Emboldened by their success at raising money wages without throwing their members out of a job (the government makes sure that that does not occur), trade union leaders become progressively more ambitious, demanding larger and larger wage increases.

The same process can also occur at less than full employment. It is by no means obvious that the overriding objective of trade union leaders is the maintenance of a maximum level of employment. If the choice confronting an individual union leader lies between on the one hand sustaining a 'high' level of employment and on the other a 'high' money wage rate, he will probably compromise, trading off employment against higher real wages. Moreover trade union leaders are in general committed to the maintenance of employment for their *own* members. They will be less concerned about the employment consequences of their actions on *other* workers. Substantial unemployment and rapid inflation can therefore co-exist on account of the selfish attitudes of those workers and their leaders who are lucky enough to remain in employment.[1]

A typical example of this view is to be found in a paper by Wiles

1. However there may come a time when the government is unwilling to continue to accommodate ever-accelerating wage settlements by providing the requisite finance. According to Kahn (1976), in a slightly different context, 'One serious aspect of the astonishing stupidity of our trade-union leaders, and of our unofficial labour leaders, is their complete failure to take a long sighted view . . . By insisting on unduly high wage increases, they force the government and the central bank to adopt restrictive measures . . .' which ultimately lead to unemployment.

(1973). In Wiles's opinion, the rate of wage inflation is determined by trade union fiat and is not susceptible to purely economic manipulation. For example, the take-over of important union positions by left-wing leaders, bent on flexing their muscles in conflict with employers, is likely to accelerate the pace of wage increase. Moreover, since prices are determined by the 'mark-up' principle by which a given increase in labour costs is passed on in the form of an equiproportionate increase in prices, the overall rate of inflation will depend upon the militancy of trade union leaders. This view has been given some degree of empirical confirmation in a controversial paper by Hines (1964), in which he pointed out the existence of a significant statistical association between the rate of wage increase and the rate of change of the proportion of the working population which is unionized. His argument is that, when trade union membership is rising, union militancy will also be increasing and hence the upward pressure upon money wages will be correspondingly higher.[2]

Leap-frogging

A more satisfactory variant of the cost-push thesis is based upon the assumption that there exists some 'fair' pattern of wage differentials which, once disturbed by some outside pressure, sets in motion a self-perpetuating process of inflation. For example, let us suppose that the economy starts off in a position of zero inflation and that it is generally agreed by all concerned that the structure of wage differentials is, in some sense, fair and equitable. Assume now that one particular labour group experiences an increase in its productivity which could be the result of capital investment, technical progress or some other factor. Let us call this group the *key* group. The workers within the key group will, quite naturally, expect a wage increase as a reward for their greater productivity. On the other hand, if other labour groups have not enjoyed similar increases in productivity, what this amounts to is an attempt by the key group of workers to upset the accepted structure of wage

2. The reader should note that many, if not most, economists do not accept Hines's results and inferences. Nor are his critics confined to the ranks of the monetarists, since they include many economists who would describe themselves as Keynesians.

differentials by leap-frogging over other groups. The wage settlement by the key group of workers will provoke retaliatory wage claims by other groups who read the initial wage claim as an unfair attempt to climb up the pecking order of differentials. To the extent (a) that the key group of workers continues to press its claim for higher *relative* wages and (b) that the threatened disruption of the fair pattern of differentials is resisted by other groups of workers, then an inflationary process will have been set in motion without any perceptible increase in the pressure of effective demand.

The basic theme of competitive leap-frogging is capable of infinite variation.[3] For example, the initial disruptive force need not be a disproportionate increase in the productivity of one group. It could easily be an *isolated* increase in the demand for one group of workers which is not generally experienced by other workers. Thus a minimal increase in the overall level of demand could, if confined to one particular labour market, lead to a substantial increase in the rate of inflation. The unifying characteristic of this diverse class of theories is the notion that the labour market is not a competitive market at all. Hicks (1975a), a pioneer in the study of the behaviour of competitive markets, has recently written: 'One is driven to the conclusion – it is, after all, a very commonsense conclusion – that there are forces at work in the determination of money wages which are non-competitive. It is just not true that money wages are determined by supply and demand.'

It will be recalled that Keynes, when discussing the reasons why the level of money wages would not decline even in the face of enormous unemployment, placed great emphasis upon the rigidity of the structure of *wage differentials* as a source of the downward inflexibility of *all* money wages (see Chapter 3, page 51). To this extent the leap-frogging theories can be seen to be in direct line of descent from Keynes's own views on the operation of the labour market. Moreover there is an impressive array of evidence, for Britain at least, that the pattern of wage differentials between different groups of workers *does* appear to be remarkably stable over quite long periods of time and despite pronounced shifts in technology and consumer preferences.

3. Two examples of the leap-frogging hypothesis are to be found in Kahn (1959 and 1975) and Hicks (1975a). Both authors are eminent Keynesians.

A further extension of this line of approach has also been proposed by Hicks (1975). This is the view that the enjoyment of full employment and steadily rising living standards since the Second World War has engendered an attitude of mind among trade union leaders which leads them to resist, not only cuts in their *money* wages, but also cuts in their *real* wages. Workers have become accustomed to high and rising real wages and will retaliate against all forces which erode the purchasing power of their money wages. Thus they will resist upward pressure on the price level just as vigorously as they have always resisted downward pressure on their money wages. This phenomenon has been labelled by Hicks *real wage resistance*.

The most frequently quoted example of how this resistance manifests itself involves the reaction of workers to increases in the cost of living brought about through rises in the prices of imported commodities. Since one of the effects of devaluation is to make imports more expensive, devaluations have often been regarded as potentially inflationary. Recent increases in the price of imported oil as a result of the OPEC cartel may be considered similarly. In both cases, the threatened deterioration in the real wage rate is resisted by means of retaliatory wage claims. To the extent that organized labour succeeds in preventing the real wage rate falling, an inflationary spiral will be set in motion with wages continually chasing prices. In addition, whatever the source of import price increases, the balance of payments will suffer under a system of fixed or quasi-fixed exchange rates: the inflationary spiral will make the economy's exports progressively more expensive and hence less competitive on international markets.[4]

A popular variant of the real wage resistance hypothesis is the 'aspirations gap' theory. Workers are assumed to form some target real wage rate on the basis of the behaviour of real wages in the recent past. For example, if post-tax real wages have usually risen at a rate of 3 per cent per annum, it is reasonable to infer that workers will come to expect future increases in post-tax real wages

4. It should be noted that the danger of devaluation leading to retaliatory wage claims underlies much of the current thinking of the New School at Cambridge.

of this order of magnitude and that, should the *actual* growth in real wages fall below the *target* growth, then wage inflation will rise. The rate of wage increase is therefore a function of the discrepancy between actual and expected real wage levels. If real wages start to grow less rapidly for external reasons (e.g. a sudden rise in the prices of imported goods), trade unions will attempt to recapture lost ground by pressing more vigorously for higher money wages (see Cripps and Godley, 1976).

But, despite the fact that there is more than a grain of truth in these aspirations gap theories, many questions remain unanswered. Firstly, there is the problem of empirical testing: given that the notion of a target real wage is a rather nebulous concept, how is it possible to devise a statistical test of this hypothesis? Do these theories come into the category of 'true but untestable' explanations of inflation (see below)? Secondly, there is a very general criticism of all cost-push theories: how can it possibly be a *rational* course of action for trade union leaders to lodge inflationary wage claims when it is clear that the living standards of their members are not materially improved, and may even be reduced, by a process of general inflation? After all, the experience of inflation should eventually convince trade union leaders that winning higher money wages does not, in itself, do much to raise the real wage rate. Trade unionists may *want* higher real wages – who does not? – but they are realistic men and understand that putting in 'excessive' wage claims is not the way to achieve this objective.

There is certainly some force in this argument when it is applied to wage bargaining in the aggregate. If wage bargaining were a highly centralized process then it should very quickly become clear to all concerned that increases in money wages over and above expected productivity growth will do nothing to raise real wages. But wage bargaining is *not* a highly centralized process: it takes place in a very ragged, discontinuous manner and involves a multiplicity of individual wage bargains, each of which has implications for other wage bargains. In other words there is nothing irrational about a leap-frogging inflationary process which, by definition, assumes a decentralized framework of collective bargaining.

How do the cost-push theorists square their interpretation of the sources of inflation with the evidence which indicates that increases in the price level tend to be positively associated with increases in the money stock? There have been few inflations of significant duration in which the stock of money did *not* increase. Why not apply the principle of Ockham's razor and accept the simplest explanation of this phenomenon, viz. the monetarist view!

Cost-push theorists, while acknowledging a fairly high degree of statistical *association* between the price level and the money stock, maintain that the direction of causation is entirely the reverse of that of the monetarist view. Instead of regarding increases in the money supply as provoking increases in the price level, the correct way to read the evidence is to view autonomous increases in money wages pushing up the price level and *calling forth* increases in the supply of money. The supply of money accommodates itself to the level of money income which, in turn, varies principally as a result of trade union pressure on wages. The central bank is assumed to act in such a way as to increase the supply of money in circulation whenever the price level rises in order to maintain full employment. Monetary policy does not play an active role in provoking inflation and is hence useless in controlling inflation. The supply of money is determined ultimately by the behaviour of money wages.

Cost-push Inflation and Economic Policy

It is not too much of an exaggeration to say that, in one form or another, the cost-push interpretation of inflation has been an essential ingredient in the 'establishment' view of economic policy in Britain since the war. True, there was a brief period in the 1960s when it was recognized that aggregate demand could *also* affect the rate of inflation, but all that this amounted to was the acknowledgement of an *additional* source of inflationary pressure. Nevertheless, the ultimate breakdown of the simple Phillips curve in the late 1960s made it possible to concentrate exclusively upon cost-push factors and to ignore the overall pressure of demand, at least as far as the rate of inflation is concerned. The three canons of this Keynesian orthodoxy were concisely summed up by Peter Jay.[5]

5. Peter Jay, *The Times*, 21 January 1976. This article is a perceptive attack on 'Keynesianism' as practised in Britain.

They are: '. . . that demand management regulates unemployment, incomes policy regulates inflation [and] the exchange rate regulates the balance of payments . . .'

Within this holy and undivided trinity we find the cure for inflation – incomes policy. According to the cost-push school, inflation arises from the defects inherent in the institutional framework of collective bargaining. Inflation can therefore be reduced only by direct intervention by the government in the process of collective bargaining in order to restore order to a situation of chaos.

The precise nature of the incomes policy depends upon the personal tastes of the economist. Those who set great store by the redistribution of national income in favour of lower-paid workers tend to prefer *flat-rate* norms such as the £6 per week limit which was enforced in Britain. Others, more conscious of the dangerous build-up of inflationary pressure which would result from too tight a compression of wage differentials, tend to prefer incomes norms expressed in *percentage* terms. Such a policy may succeed in scaling down the overall pace of wage inflation without at the same time disturbing the time-honoured pattern of 'fair' differentials.

The Difficulties of Discriminating between Cost and Demand Inflation

When one considers the evidence on the inflationary experience of an individual national economy, the difficulty of distinguishing between cost and demand influences would appear to be insuperable. How is one to choose between, on the one hand, a view of inflation which attributes a central initiating role to the supply of money; and, on the other, one which focuses upon the autonomous monopolistic forces which put continuous upward pressure on wages and prices irrespective of the pressure of demand and which are underwritten by the accommodating actions of the monetary authorities? The evidence would appear to be capable of a considerable latitude of interpretation. Whereas monetarists regard the causal relation between the money supply and the price level as running from the former to the latter, cost-push theorists argue that the direction of causation is in fact the opposite, running from a politically/sociologically determined price level to a passive actor, the supply of money. Whether one subscribes to a monetarist or a cost-push view of inflation depends, therefore, upon one's personal reading of the evidence. Do trade unions exert an overwhelming pressure upon the level of money wages independently of market conditions or do they merely rubber-stamp wage contracts which would have been arrived at in the market-place in any case?

On a purely national basis, no single piece of evidence exists to clinch the argument one way or the other. Orthodox monetarists continue to insist that an 'expectations-augmented' Phillips curve does in fact exist while other researchers (e.g. Henry, Sawyer and Smith, 1976) can find no trace of such a relationship.

But monetarists claim that this deadlock is broken when one remembers that the recent inflation was an international phenomenon, afflicting a wide variety of countries with very different sociopolitical backgrounds simultaneously. True, not all countries were inflating at the same rate, but no theory predicts precise equality between individual national inflation rates. The extraordinary rise in the world-wide rate of inflation after about 1968 must surely pose an important challenge to any theory of inflation. How do the two polar extreme theories of inflation explain the fact that the recent inflation has been a world-wide phenomenon?

Excess Demand Explanations

Monetarists believe that the increases in the inflation rate experienced by the western trading bloc can be explained *principally* in terms of the increase in the world supply of money which largely resulted from the balance of payments deficit of the United States. When a country starts running a balance of payments deficit, it pays out more for its imports than it receives from abroad in payment for its exports. If that country is as economically dominant as the United States, it can finance its payments deficit by issuing dollars to foreigners. Moreover, since the dollar is the most readily acceptable currency in the western trading bloc, foreigners will be perfectly willing to accept payment for their exports (US imports) in terms of dollars. Nevertheless the impact on the rest of the world of the continual injection of dollars into their respective economies will be to provoke inflation, for unless it is counteracted by the policies of the individual monetary authorities the effect of the dollar deficit is very similar to domestic credit creation by the central banks of the rest of the world.

The repercussions for the rest of the world of the dollar deficit can also be analysed in simple Keynesian terms. If imports are regarded as a withdrawal from the level of effective demand (similar to savings) and exports are regarded as an injection (similar to investment), an increase in the flow of exports over imports resulting from the American balance of payments deficit will lead to a net injection of effective demand into the economies of the rest of the world. This would produce an expansion in aggregate demand in just the same way as an increase in government spending would do in a closed economy. If the economies of the rest of the world are at or near full employment, the increase in effective demand will open up an inflationary gap which, by definition, drives the price level upwards. This upward pressure on the price level will persist for as long as the economies of the rest of the world continue to run a net balance of payments surplus with America. Moreover the inflationary gap in the rest of the world is not matched by a corresponding deflationary gap in the United States because of the *inflationary method of finance* of the American balance of payments deficit. Now payments deficits need not be inflationary if they are financed by borrowing from the rest of the world: in this case the US deficit would not in itself produce inflation in the rest of the world since capital movements (loans) from the rest of the world would recirculate demand pressure back to America. On the other hand if the United States chose to exploit the dominant position of the dollar as the principal reserve currency, it could finance the deficit in an *inflationary* manner by issuing new money to foreigners. This new money would indeed be inflationary since it represents a net injection of effective demand into the world economy.[6]

6. More extreme monetarists often blame the world-wide inflation upon the pursuit of 'Keynesian' policies by the American demand-management authorities. This view is based upon the identification of 'Keynesianism' with indiscriminate expansionism.

Whether one prefers to analyse there sponse of the world economy to an American payments deficit financed by the issue of new money in monetarist or Keynesian terms is a matter of personal preference. Both approaches predict the same outcome, namely, inflationary pressure, generated in the United States and disseminated (within a system of fairly inflexible exchange rates) throughout the rest of the world. In a highly interdependent world economy, inflationary pressure is no respecter of national boundaries. Nonetheless, a vital assumption of this explanation of world inflation is that the rest of the world was initially in a state of full employment.

Cost-Push Explanations

Unlike the excess-demand hypothesis, the cost-push hypothesis of inflation is very ill-suited to provide a quantitatively testable explanation of the phenomenon of world-wide inflation. This has led many monetarists to criticize the cost-push hypothesis for being 'unscientific'. One prominent monetarist has gone so far as to accuse the cost-push school of practising 'bad economics' (Laidler, 1974): in order to be 'meaningful', propositions concerning the causes of economic phenomena should be empirically testable by econometric or other techniques of analysis. But this is surely a harsh judgment on a hypothesis which is accepted by many economists with impeccable analytical credentials. Indeed one of the most perceptive critiques of the 'scientism' of much of modern economics is to be found in the writings of Professor Hayek, who in other respects is greatly admired in monetarist circles. According to Hayek many of the most important propositions in economics, while being in some sense 'true', are intrinsically untestable. And even if one accepts the claim that only statistically testable propositions can be counted as 'meaningful', what becomes of the scientific status of the monetarist 'rising natural unemployment rate' hypothesis?

Nevertheless some cost-push theorists have at least recognized the necessity for squaring the facts of international economic experience with the experience of an individual economy (normally the British economy, where such theories are particularly thick on the ground). Though the cost-push view of the origins of world-wide inflation varies from economist to economist, there is general agreement with the views expressed by Wiles (1973). Wiles maintains that the international upsurge of inflationary pressure after 1968 can be traced directly to such socio-political sources as the Paris riots and mini-revolution of 1968, the general growth of left-wing agitation and militancy within trade unions, the spilling over of the criterion of comparability to encompass inter-country wage rivalry (French workers, jealous of the standard of living of West German workers, are presumed to attempt to achieve this same standard of living by making a wage claim of appropriate magnitude). The list can be extended more or less indefinitely.

How are we to interpret the general world-wide reduction in the rate of inflation which has occurred since around 1974? Has the class struggle become less intense? The annual rioting season in French universities is still with us. Have French workers ceased to strive for the living standards of their German or Japanese colleagues? Is there any indication that 'moderate' trade union leaders have ousted their leftist rivals in the economies of the western trading bloc? These are questions which the cost-push hypothesis finds very difficult to answer.

The Kaldor Hypothesis

A far more satisfactory and analytically complete explanation of the world-wide inflation has been proposed by Nicholas Kaldor (1976). Kaldor rejects the excess demand explanation of inflation outlined previously since it critically depends upon the assumption of full employment in the rest of the world. Now while it may have been the case that *some* economies were operating at more or less full employment levels of activity, it was by no means generally true. For example, the British wage explosion of 1969/70 took place against the background of a relatively high unemployment rate. Indeed it became evident in 1970 that the economy was moving into recession. In other words it is very difficult to attribute the post-1969 inflation to excess aggregate demand.

Kaldor's explanation of the post-1969 acceleration of inflation rests upon five principal assumptions: (a) the prices of primary commodities, excluding oil and some kinds of food, are mainly determined by the forces of world supply and demand; (b) the price of oil is determined by the OPEC cartel which will act like the monopoly supplier of any other commodity, attempting to maximize profit but at the same time not wishing to 'spoil' the market for oil by inflicting excessive damage on the economies of its principal customers: but within these broad constraints the OPEC cartel has considerable freedom of manoeuvre and can (and did) increase the price of oil very steeply; (c) the prices of many other commodities (e.g. agricultural products within the EEC) have their prices fixed by bureaucratic fiat irrespective of demand conditions – hence all the butter mountains and wine lakes; (d) the prices of *industrial* commodities are largely cost-determined, the most important costs being money wages and the prices of raw materials; (e) superimposed upon the leap-frogging mechanism, which mainly accounted for the 'creeping' inflation of the 1950s and 1960s, is the Hicks phenomenon of real wage resistance.

The rapid acceleration of inflation in the early 1970s can be explained (1) by the explosion of commodity prices as a result of world-wide excess demand for these goods; (2) by the quadrupling of oil prices by the OPEC cartel; (3) by the increase in the prices of agricultural goods in some countries (e.g. Britain) as a result of the operation of agricultural price support schemes. As far as item (1) is concerned, the rise in the prices of commodities produced under competitive conditions led to an improvement in the terms of trade[7] for primary producers and should have also led to a channelling of capital and other resources into primary production: the supply of primary commodities should have risen and the terms of trade for industrial goods should have made a modest recovery as a result. The main snag with this mechanism is that, since primary commodities are inputs into the process by which industrial goods are produced and since industrial prices are set at a mark-up over production costs, the rise in the prices of primary commodities raises the prices of industrial goods also. Once the prices of industrial goods start to rise more rapidly than before, workers, fearful lest their standard of living be eroded by price inflation, lodge compensatory wage claims: the phenomenon of real wage resistance leads to an increase in the rate of wage in-

7. In this context the terms of trade is the ratio of an index of industrial prices to an index of the prices of non-industrial commodities.

flation which, in turn, feeds back to the cost of production of industrial commodities. A 'primary price/industrial price/money wage rate' spiral will have been triggered off or aggravated. This spiral will increase in momentum once inflationary expectations start to build up. In this mechanism the change in the terms of trade in favour of primary products led to a vicious spiral of inflation. Indeed if real wage resistance is absolute, the eventual build-up of inflationary expectations will lead to an explosive inflationary process. Add to this the considerable increase in the prices of oil and (in the case of Britain) agricultural products and an extra dimension is added to the above spiral.

But Kaldor's hypothesis is not only interesting for the way it explains the recent world-wide inflation: it also points to the causes of the simultaneous rise in inflation and the growing world recession, a phenomenon which the monetarist model is very ill-equipped to analyse. Kaldor proposes two main reasons for the general rise in unemployment and the decline in growth rates in the 1970s. (1) The large increase in the value of the exports of oil-producing countries was not matched by a rise in their imports. The appearance of this imbalance led to a world-wide fall in effective demand for manufactured goods. (2) The widespread implementation of restrictive demand-management policies to cure an inflation that had not been caused by excess demand for the products of *industrial* countries in the first place. The first reason is quite easily grasped: windfall profits accrued to commodity producers but only a part of this increase in profits resulted in higher spending, the rest being saved. The second reason reflects the fact that misguided policies were adopted to cure inflation in a large number of countries. But since the inflation had not been caused by excessive aggregate demand (except perhaps for primary commodities other than oil and food), it made little sense for government to try to reduce inflation by implementing deflationary policies. The fact that many countries did in fact implement such policies needlessly raised unemployment still further but did nothing to cure inflation. Clearly this argument only holds good if the factor which triggered off the inflationary spiral was a substantial increase in *administered* prices (e.g. the price of oil or the prices of those agricultural products fixed by the price support schemes of the EEC). It does not hold good if the initiating factor was a rise in competitively priced commodities, since a fall in the world-wide demand for all goods induced by restrictive demand-management policies will reduce the prices – or the rate of increase of the prices – of these commodities.

Asymmetry in Inflationary Processes

We have now encountered two diametrically opposed interpretations of the causes of inflation. On the one hand there is the excess expenditure school, the most vocal members of which are the monetarists, who trace inflation to present or past laxity in the implementation of monetary and fiscal policies and who recommend a policy of deliberate but temporary under-utilization of capacity in order to bring inflation under control. The 'temporariness' of such a policy is a matter of some dispute, a typical estimate being a period of under-utilization of two to five years. Moreover the monetarist wing of this school insists that demand restriction is both a necessary *and a sufficient condition* for the taming of the inflationary tiger. Other policies for controlling inflation, in particular prices and incomes policies, are at best useless and are most probably positively harmful, since they will impede the functioning of the price mechanism. It is in their dismissal of incomes policies that the free-market commitment of most monetarists comes to the surface.

On the other side is the cost-push school whose views we have outlined above. According to this school, governments should not abandon their full-employment commitment in order to bring inflation under control. Not only would such a policy be highly wasteful in terms of lost output and socially disruptive as a result of the necessarily high level of unemployment which it entails, it would also be ineffective. Since the origins of inflation are to be found in the competitive power struggles within and between different social groups which are independent of the latent forces of supply and demand, the application of 'market' solutions to the problem of inflation, as the monetarists advocate, will fail to reduce the rate of inflation.

116

One can scarcely conceive of two more contrary interpretations of the same phenomenon. Nevertheless, whatever one's opinion regarding the causes of inflation, it is surely essential to recognize that an inflationary process is likely to be asymmetrical. In particular, even if one accepts the view that inflation was caused by past 'laxity' in the conduct of macroeconomic policy, it does not follow that a policy of demand restriction alone will succeed in reducing the pace of inflation if the rate of change of money wages is inflexible in a downward direction. (This observation applies *a fortiori* if one accepts a cost-push view of inflation.)

The Downward Inflexibility of the Rate of Increase of Wages

At the time when Keynes wrote the *General Theory*, the level of prices and money wages had remained roughly constant for a considerable period of time. We have seen how Keynes explained the sources of this wage rigidity in terms of the great importance of preserving the structure of wage differentials. A widespread excess supply of labour would not lead to reductions in the *general* level of money wages, for such a general wage reduction would require the concerted and simultaneous reduction in a whole set of individual money wage rates.[8] Moreover each trade union leader, jealously defending the wage differentials between his own members and members of other groups of workers, will be unwilling to take the first step and accept a money wage cut for fear of endangering his members' relative position in the structure of pay differentials.

Now exactly the same arguments are, in principle, applicable to a situation in which a positive rate of wage increase is being experienced. If trade union leaders are obsessed with the preservation of received differentials, then an overall excess supply of labour, deliberately produced by the actions of the demand-management authorities, will probably not result in a general reduction in the *rate of change* of money wages. Once again a general retardation of the pace of wage increase in the presence of involuntary unemployment requires a simultaneous reduction in the scale of a whole series of wage increases. Since each union leader is reluctant to take the first step, and possibly endanger the relative position of

8. See Chapter 3, p. 51.

his members, an overall reduction in the rate of wage inflation is unlikely to occur to any significant extent. Hence all that restrictive demand-management policies succeed in doing is to raise the unemployment rate; they do very little to temper the pace of inflation.

Anti-Inflation Policy

Let us *assume* that the monetarists are correct when they claim that inflation is the result of misguided attempts to 'over-utilize' capacity by the demand-management authorities. In the light of the above observation concerning the downward rigidity of the rate of change of money wages, a policy of relying on demand restriction alone to cure inflation would appear to be very inadequate indeed. Reductions in the overall level of demand will produce substantial increases in the unemployment rate but relatively small (perhaps verging on the imperceptible) reductions in the rate of wage and price increases. Monetarists place an excessive amount of faith in their assumption that the labour market reacts to slack demand in exactly the opposite direction to its response to excess demand. The asymmetry between expansionary and contractionary processes is an important missing ingredient in a monetarist interpretation of inflation (there are many more which have already been touched upon). The recognition of this asymmetry owing to 'ratchet' effects is of considerable practical importance when it comes to devising the appropriate set of economic policies to control inflation.

In the author's opinion a policy for prices and incomes control is indispensable to any strategy for reducing the rate of inflation. At the very least such a policy would, if it were believed in by the public, directly reduce the anticipated rate of inflation, thereby taking much of the urgency out of the process of collective bargaining. But, more than this, it would aim at eliminating that very considerable part of a process of inflation which can be attributed to autonomous wage push. The monetarist claim that such policies impair the allocative efficiency of the labour market by interfering with 'relative price signals' is greatly exaggerated: there is a great deal of evidence to support the view that the structure of wage differentials (the 'relative prices' that monetarists are usually referring to) is highly rigid over time. Imposing constraints on a

118

structure of wages which is already inflexible will produce very little extra misallocation of resources. It must be admitted, however, that the track record of prices and incomes policies, particularly in Britain, is not very distinguished; but recognition of this undeniable fact should not lead to the over-reaction in favour of 'market' cures for inflation which has occurred in recent years.

The main practical difficulty associated with the implementation of incomes policies rests in the degree of flexibility that the policy should possess. On the one hand there are those who believe in the 'rough justice' principle whereby a given norm is applied across the board and no exceptional cases are allowed for. This approach has the advantage of simplicity and also of closing up many of the loop-holes which may tend to undermine a more loosely framed policy. On the other hand, there are those who believe that an incomes policy, while laying down basic norms (expressed either in percentage or flat-rate terms) should also make provision for exceptional circumstances so that the price mechanism is not entirely stifled. It is occasionally necessary, they argue, that certain groups be awarded pay increases in excess of the basic norm. For example, if it can be shown that certain groups of workers have achieved higher than average productivity increases, or that other groups are in particular demand, then these groups should be allowed to claim wage increases over and above the awards to other groups. If this policy were successful the wage structure would become *more* flexible under a system of prices and incomes restraint than it had been under a system of 'free' collective bargaining. But the very real danger in this approach is that too many groups of workers may start to regard themselves as special cases, rendering the basic norm an irrelevant concept. Moreover the success of this policy depends upon the willingness of the trade unions to allow differentials to vary much more freely than they have in the past.

The choice between rigid or flexible policies and flat-rate or percentage norms is fundamentally political in nature. All that the economist can do is to point out to the decision maker the likely economic consequences of one or other line of action.

Chapter 8
Economic Policy and Inflation

The Position So Far

We are now in a position to draw together some of the threads of the previous discussion and assess the state of play between the monetarist, the Keynesian and the cost-push views of the nature of the inflationary process.

Monetarists

Monetarists regard inflation as being the outcome of past or present laxity in the conduct of monetary policy by the responsible authorities. They recommend the implementation of a policy of gradual but determined reductions in the rate of increase in monetary expansion so as to erode inflationary expectations by continually displacing the short-run Phillips curve in a south-westerly direction. Since the erosion of inflationary expectations can only be achieved by the generation of a deflationary gap by the monetary authorities, any successful strategy for controlling inflation will necessarily involve a considerable period of under-utilization of capacity. This will necessitate running the economy at a pressure of demand such that the actual unemployment rate exceeds the natural rate. Gradually, however, as market forces chip away at inflationary expectations, producing reductions in the actual rate of inflation, the unemployment rate can be allowed to edge back towards its natural rate. Once inflation has been conquered, or at least reduced to tolerable proportions, the role of the monetary authorities will be to keep a constant check over the growth of the money stock, making sure that it is not allowed to increase by more than the rate of growth of output (ignoring for simplicity long-run changes in velocity). The usual rider must be added to allow for the rational expectations variant of monetarism which claims that the extent of under-utilization of capacity and 'unnatural' unemployment will be much less than orthodox monetarists think to be the case. Indeed they argue that pre-announced money supply targets, if they are believed by the public at large, will have a fairly immediate, direct impact upon the price level and the rate of inflation. If public confidence in the firmness of the government's resolve to hold to the monetary targets is strong, there will only be a minimal reduction in aggregate demand.

Prices and incomes policies have no role to play in most of the monetarist writings on inflation. Indeed such policies are viewed with considerable hostility since they are held to be unwelcome in-trusions into the functioning of the market mechanism. Monetar-ists argue that the harmful side-effects upon the allocation of resources which result when arbitrary administrative rules are imposed more than outweigh the supposed benefits of prices and incomes policies as instruments for controlling inflation.

In the opinion of the present author, the cavalier dismissal of incomes policies by monetarists is unwarranted. Although there is a very real danger of some distortion in the allocation of resources if too rigid an incomes policy were implemented for too long a period of time, it is not at all clear that the costs of a sufficiently flexible incomes policy would be all that great when judged in relation to the benefits of a more rapid reduction in the rate of inflation. Indeed even according to the internal logic of the mone-tarists' own position, policies which accelerate the downward revision of inflationary expectations are to be welcomed, provided, of course, that the detrimental side-effects of such policies are not deemed to be excessive. To the extent that incomes policies are (or should be) expressly devised to perform such a role, it is unfortu-nate that monetarists should have ruled these policies out of court. Moreover, despite the superficial plausibility of the monetarist objection to incomes policies, it is by no means obvious that the wage structure allocates labour in a manner predicted by com-petitive theory. The pattern of wage differentials, even during periods of 'free' collective bargaining, appears to be highly inflex-ible. A sufficiently imaginative incomes policy could conceivably succeed in 'loosening up' the structure of differentials as well as

121

reducing the overall rate of inflation. Such a policy would, in fact, be facilitating the operation of the market mechanism rather than impeding it.

The Cost-Push View

At the other extreme is the cost-push interpretation of the inflationary process. This is a heterogeneous collection of theories, including at one end the relatively plausible 'leap-frogging' theories of trade union behaviour and at the other the 'class-struggle' theories which view inflation as the true crisis in capitalism (it used to be unemployment). The unifying feature of this group of theories is that the process of inflation cannot be analysed according to the classic economic principles of supply and demand. Rising prices are not the outcome of the excessive demand. It is true that an inflationary process requires the continual injection of money by the central bank so as to prevent the emergence of widespread unemployment, but this should not lead to the erroneous inference that the increases in the money supply *caused* the inflation. Cost-push theorists argue that the money supply responds passively to prior changes in the price level which are in turn determined by socio-political factors beyond the terms of reference of traditional economic analysis.

Cost-push remedies for inflation are as numerous as the original theories. In general, however, the essential ingredient of an anti-inflation programme must, according to the cost-push school, be an incomes policy. Whereas many economists now accept that incomes policies may have an important *short-run* role to play in bringing inflation under control, some adherents of the cost-push view go further than this by recommending a *permanent* policy of prices and incomes restraint. Naturally restrictive demand-management policies are rarely mentioned with any approval, since the manipulation of aggregate demand principally affects the level of employment. Cost-push theorists reject the proposition that a policy of restricting aggregate demand affects *both* the unemployment rate *and* the rate of inflation.

The Keynesian View

Occupying the distinctly uncomfortable middle-ground between these two warring factions are the Keynesians. According to the analysis of Chapters 6 and 7, the Keynesian position, as interpreted by the present author, can be summarized as follows:

(a) *If* inflation is caused by excess demand, as it may be during wartime or during peacetime booms in activity, then by all means implement a policy of demand restriction. On the other hand, if, as seems likely for most countries during more normal times, the upward pressure on wages and prices comes from non-competitive sources, then a policy of demand restriction will be worse than useless. But in both cases a policy of prices and incomes control is necessary: in the first case in order to assist demand restriction in eroding inflationary expectations; in the second case as the only cure for inflation which has a chance of succeeding.

(b) Even if it were accepted that excess demand caused the inflations experienced since the Second World War – and many respected Keynesians firmly reject this view – the monetarist claim that demand restriction can most effectively be implemented by means of monetary as opposed to fiscal control is groundless since it ignores the crucial relationship between the actions of the fiscal authorities and the behaviour of the money supply. Once the relation between the financing of a budget deficit and the size of the money stock is appreciated, many of the time-honoured points of conflict between Keynesians and monetarists are found to be without substance. Of particular importance in this context is the two-stage process for manipulating the level of aggregate demand which Keynes eventually proposed in the late 1930s but which has been largely ignored ever since.

(c) Reductions in the pressure of demand, engineered through restrictive fiscal and open-market policies, though they may be a necessary ingredient in an anti-inflation package, will not be sufficient, at least in relation to the time-scale on which most democratic governments are forced to operate. The existence of important rigidities in the process of collective bargaining may render the rate of change of money wages highly unresponsive to reductions in the pressure of demand. This is not to say that the rate of wage inflation is totally inflexible, merely that it behaves very differently in the upswing of the cycle from in the downswing. If such an asymmetry is present then it becomes all the more urgent to devise

123

direct methods of reducing the scale of money wage increases. It is for this reason that a policy of prices and incomes control becomes an even more vital element in a Keynesian package to control inflation.

International Inflation: To Float or Not to Float

Let us assume that the government has implemented the policies of (perhaps) demand restriction and (definitely) prices and incomes control which were recommended above, and that both sets of policies have been successful in reducing the domestic rate of inflation below the rates of the country's international competitors. How is this government to defend its anti-inflation programme against the general price increases which may be occurring in the rest of the world? The traditional answer to this question is that the government should float the currency in order to isolate its economy from world-wide inflationary pressure. In such circumstances the discrepancy between the domestic and foreign rates of inflation will result in the continual upward drift of the exchange rate. One wing of the monetarist camp has objected to this traditional position, arguing that the knowledge that it can float the currency downwards if the need arises may lessen the government's resolve to adopt the appropriate monetary policies to control inflation. Finally there is the cost-push position, which views floating (more particularly downward floating) with suspicion since the rise in import prices which would result from a depreciation of the currency would add a further twist to an already vicious wage-price spiral.

The Arguments for Floating the Currency

Let us assume that there are only two countries in the world, America and Britain, and that both countries are in balance of payments equilibrium in the sense that the value of each country's imports is exactly equal to the value of its exports (capital movements are ignored). If America now adopts expansionary monetary and fiscal policies, its balance of payments will run into deficit both on account of the sucking in of imports to enable production to rise and also on account of the decline of the competitiveness of its exports as a result of the domestic inflation which will be produced. The mirror image of the American payments deficit is a British payments surplus of equal magnitude: British exports exceed its imports by exactly the same amount as American imports exceed its exports.

Under the *gold standard*, the American payments deficit would have led to a flow of gold out of America into Britain. This would produce two effects, both of which would ultimately lead to the restoration of international balance of payments equilibrium. The first would be deflation in America, leading to a temporary fall in output and employment and a consequent reduction in the flow of imports into America. American exports would also regain some of their former competitiveness to the extent that American wages and prices fell (or rose less rapidly) in response to the deflationary gap. The second effect would be inflation in Britain as a result of the inflow of gold into Britain. This would produce an inflationary gap, a rise in the flow of imports and a deterioration in the international competitiveness of British exports. Thus excess demand in Britain and excess supply in America both evoke responses which eventually lead to the re-establishment of payments equilibrium in each country. The prime motive force was the flow of gold from America to Britain and the adjustment mechanism consisted of the quantity theory of money applied to the international economy.

Now of course modern international monetary affairs are no longer conducted according to the principles of the gold standard. At the risk of oversimplification, we may say that the role of gold has been largely assumed by the dollar, which is the principal reserve currency in the western trading bloc. As we saw in Chapter 7, if America ran a payments deficit with Britain, it could either finance this deficit in a non-inflationary manner by borrowing from Britain (hard to conceive nowadays) or it could exploit the dollar's position as the dominant reserve currency and issue new dollars, thus swelling the total stock of dollars in the world. This latter method of finance is distinctly inflationary and has been blamed by monetarists for a large part of the recent inflation.

What effect does floating the exchange rate have upon the prob-

125

lem of international monetary adjustment? The exchange rate between the pound and the dollar is the number of dollars for which one pound sterling can be exchanged on the foreign-exchange market. It is the *dollar price* of one pound sterling. Now the market for currency functions in just the same way as any other market, responding to changes in underlying supply and demand conditions through variations in the exchange rate (provided, of course, that the authorities allow these variations to take place). Thus when there is an excess demand for sterling, its price in terms of dollars will rise, and vice versa when there is an excess supply.[1]

To return to our former example, if the American authorities decided to pursue expansive monetary and fiscal policies at home, under a régime of floating exchange rates they would not be able to foist extra dollar holdings on Britain, for the increase in the supply of dollars on the foreign-exchange market would simply serve to depress the exchange rate between the dollar and the pound sterling (i.e. to revalue sterling). A balance of payments deficit could only occur if the American (or British) monetary authorities attempted to intervene in order to prevent the value of the dollar from falling to its market-clearing price. One advantage for Britain of a system of floating exchange rates is that it is protected from the spill-over of inflationary pressure from America which would occur under a system of fixed or quasi-fixed exchange rates. Furthermore, it brings home to the American authorities the need to put their own house in order for they are now unable to export inflationary pressure to Britain through its balance of payments deficit.

It has been argued that one of the principal advantages of a system of floating exchange rates is that it lifts the shadow of the balance of payments from the arena of domestic economic management. Many commentators believe that, if an open economy is to

1. Central banks have often been reluctant to stand on the side-lines and merely spectate in the face of what they regard as unduly erratic fluctuations in the exchange rates for their currency. For example, the Bank of England has often intervened to support what it considers to be a reasonable price for sterling by running down its gold and foreign-currency reserves in order to create an additional demand for sterling when there would otherwise be a downward drift in the exchange rate. In this way central banks have attempted to iron out unnecessary, though potentially disruptive, ripples in exchange rates. This intervention is often referred to as 'dirty floating'.

enjoy the benefits of full employment while at the same time being deprived of the option of altering its exchange rate, the price may be a prolonged balance of payments deficit, since the flow of imports which would be necessary to maintain output at its full-employment level would chronically exceed the flow of exports from that economy.[2] Every time the authorities attempt to raise the level of economic activity and reduce the unemployment rate, the balance of payments runs into deficit, which in turn leads to the reversal of the expansionary policies. The balance of payments has therefore often been regarded as a barrier to full employment. Indeed this was the view held by Keynes in the early 1920s when he was arguing against the revaluation of sterling against the dollar. A flexible exchange rate removes this barrier by allowing the currency to float downwards as full employment is approached, thus preventing a widening of the gap between imports and exports.[3] It is only misguided attempts to maintain an overvalued currency that introduce any conflict between balance of payments equilibrium and full employment.

The Monetarist Case Against Floating

Whereas up to fairly recently the vast majority of monetarists were in favour of the free floating of individual currencies, the advocacy of a modified version of the gold standard (or gold-exchange standard) has re-emerged among monetarists. The redoubtable Professor Friedrich von Hayek, a former sparring partner of Keynes in the 1930s, has returned to the macroeconomic fray with a vengeance. Hayek (1975) has argued vigorously in favour of the maintenance of *fixed* exchange rates between trading partners on the grounds that they impose a rigid discipline upon the domestic actions of governments who may be tempted to follow the inflationist path in their monetary and fiscal policies. Despite their high-minded promises to bring inflation under control through constant vigilance over the supply of money, governments simply cannot be trusted. In most democratic countries governments are

2. A similar view is held by the Cambridge Economic Policy Group, although this group is not particularly enthusiastic about floating.

3. This statement assumes that the *Marshall–Lerner* condition holds. This is an issue of some complexity which cannot be pursued at this point.

under continual pressure from all sides to undertake expenditure projects which are ultimately inflationary. Despite their publicly avowed resolve to hold the line on the money supply, there is a high probability of their succumbing to this pressure, secure in the knowledge that at least the balance of payments will not suffer since the brunt of the inflationary burden will be borne by a downward drift of the exchange rate. Floating exchange rates therefore furnish pusillanimous governments with an escape route by which to avoid the detrimental effect that inflationary domestic policies would otherwise have upon the balance of payments.

On the other hand fixed exchange rates, according to Hayek, do not offer the same temptation to governments to behave irresponsibly in their domestic monetary policies. If governments fall by the wayside and resort to inflationary financial practices, the rapid deterioration in the balance of payments, reflected in the outflow of gold and foreign exchange reserves, would quickly lead to the reversal of such policies. To the extent that it was based upon the objective of fixed exchange rates, Hayek applauds the Bretton Woods system of international adjustment, though he has reservations on other aspects of the agreement. The breakdown of the Bretton Woods agreement in the late 1960s, when country after country decided to float, albeit dirtily, removed the last obstacle to national – and hence international – inflation. Commenting on the future of the international monetary system, Hayek writes:

... in the long run I do not believe we shall regain a system of international stability without returning to a system of fixed exchange rates which imposes upon the national central banks the restraint essential if they are successfully to resist the pressure of the inflation-minded forces of their countries – usually including Ministers of Finance.

Although there may be something to be said for constraining the room for manoeuvre of the domestic monetary authorities, Hayek surely underestimates the very considerable hostility with which the voting public regards *both* domestic inflation *and* the depreciation of the currency. At the time of writing, the unemployment rate in Britain stands at its highest level for thirty years and shows every sign of increasing still further. Nevertheless there is every indication that the general public is right behind the Chancellor of the Exchequer in his anti-inflation programme. Even trade union leaders, despite the occasional call for selective reflation, have co-operated to a significant extent in the overall strategy to control inflation. Hayek fails to recognize the widespread unpopularity both of inflation and currency depreciation and the effect of this unpopularity upon those who fashion our economic policies.

Moreover, even if one were to share Hayek's scepticism regarding the determination of governments to control the growth of the money supply, is his proposed return to a system of rigidly fixed exchange rates the *only* method of enforcing discipline upon back-sliding governments? Other writers have advocated less drastic methods of imposing restraint on the monetary authorities. For example, Professors Rowley and Peacock (1975) have recommended a legally enforceable framework in which all governmental control over the money supply is completely eliminated. Writing in similar vein Peter Jay (1976) has proposed the setting up of a Currency Commission which would

... be required by statute to regulate the growth of the money supply ... so that in no 12-month period does it depart by more than 2 percentage points from the long term growth of the productive potential of the economy as estimated from time to time either by the commissioners or by a suitably designated advisory body of competent economists appointed by the commission.

Once the growth in the money supply has been adjusted to the long-term rate of economic growth, the supposedly detrimental effects of collective bargaining will manifest themselves not in rising prices, but in higher unemployment, through just the same mechanism as any other form of monopolistic price-setting.

Floating and the Cost-Push School

The cost-push attitude towards floating currencies is, predictably, luke warm. If the rate of inflation of a particular country (normally Britain) exceeds that of its international competitors, its balance of payments will deteriorate. Allowing the currency to depreciate will have the effect of making exports more competitive and will, other things being equal, serve to close the balance of payments deficit. The problem is that other things do not remain equal. More specifically, while a depreciation of the currency makes exports cheaper, it also makes imports more expensive. According to standard (i.e. neo-classical) theory, this will, in the longer term, lead to a further improvement in the balance of payments, since domestic demand will be diverted away from imported goods towards domestically produced *import substitutes*.

In the short term, however, the rise in import prices will raise the overall price level. If, as many adherents of the cost-push hypothesis believe, workers are prepared to defend their real living standards from all forms of attack, then they will simply respond to this depreciation-induced rise in the cost of living by lodging compensatory wage claims. Indeed the additional increase in the price level brought about through the downward drift in the value of the currency will add further momentum to the inflationary spiral, since union leaders will have to put in even larger wage claims in order to prevent the erosion of their members' living standards. The stage is then set for further increases in the rate of inflation: inflation leads to a depreciation of the currency, which leads to a higher rate of inflation, which, in turn, leads to a further depreciation of the currency. If real wage resistance is absolute (i.e. workers are unwilling to tolerate *any* reduction in their real standard of life) this spiral of inflation will explode, hyperinflation being the ultimate outcome.

The inflationary repercussions of devaluations are emphasized by the Cambridge Economic Policy Group, often referred to as the New School at Cambridge. This group argues that only quite massive devaluations – perhaps of the order of 40 per cent – will have much effect in stimulating the production and sale of exports and of import substitutes to such an extent that output growth could be sustained, while at the same time the balance of payments deficit is reduced or eliminated altogether. However, this solution to the problem of how to achieve reasonable employment levels without inflation and payments deficits is riddled with snags, the most intractable of which is the likely breakdown of the incomes policy – which the New School sees as an important instrument for containing inflation – as a result of retaliation by workers against the large increase in import prices which such a drastic devaluation would necessarily entail. If workers press for *full* compensation for the rise in import prices, then even a huge devaluation will fail to shift resources towards the production of exports and import substitutes.

For this reason the New School argues in favour of direct controls on imports. Import controls would achieve all of the beneficial results of a *successful* devaluation – higher employment, higher output and rising real wages – but would have a far greater chance of *actually* succeeding than a large devaluation. The reason for the higher chance of success of import controls hinges upon the fact that they will serve to reduce the real wage by much less than would a devaluation (at least in its initial stages). Indeed real wages will, in fact, be able to rise as a result of the rise in output that would take place behind the protective barrier of import controls. If this were to occur, then a rise in employment would be accompanied by lower and not higher inflation: workers are less inclined to lodge 'excessive' wage claims when their standard of living is rising, or at least constant, than when it is falling (see the 'aspirations gap' theories of inflation in Chapter 7). The incomes policy which the New School regards as a desirable ingredient of macroeconomic control would therefore be less likely to be undermined by cost-push forces.

The New School at Cambridge is not oblivious of the undesirable consequences of import controls. It does not seek to minimize the detrimental effects on, for example, the freedom of choice of the consumer (at least in the short run) of the imposition of such controls. After all, is it reasonable to expect the British consumer to restrict his purchases of motor cars to British models which he considers, for whatever reason, to be inferior to Japanese cars? Nevertheless the New School sees import controls as playing an essential role in arresting the process of de-industrialization in Britain.

Indexation

One further method of reducing the rate of inflation has gained considerable popularity in recent years, particularly among monetarists. This is the implementation of a policy of *indexation* of nominal contracts, that is the provision of escalator clauses in money contracts which guard against price increases which occur after the date of commencement of the contractual agreement. For example, a wage bargain could be struck between workers and employers whereby a wage rate of, say, £70 per week would be payable until the next round of wage negotiations if no price increases occur; and a wage rate of £70 plus an inflation premium would be payable should positive inflation occur. In other words, the wage contract would be made inflation-proof by the automatic guarantee of a given real wage rate over the period of the wage bargain. The money wage rate would be automatically linked to the price index.

In principle, index-linked contracts can be applied over a wide range of economic activity. For example, taxes could be indexed so as to avoid the phenomenon of fiscal drag whereby government tax receipts rise in real value purely as a result of inflation, on account of the fact that personal allowances are at present denominated in money terms and that the taxation system is progressive. As inflation pushes more workers into higher tax brackets, their real tax bill also rises since a higher proportion of their money incomes are being appropriated by the government in the form of tax payments.

Similarly the interest payments in debtor–creditor contracts could be linked to subsequent changes in the cost of living. If both debtor and creditor agreed to a real interest payment of 4 per cent per annum and the rate of inflation over the following year turned out to be 7 per cent, then the money rate of interest actually payable at the end of the year would be 11 per cent. The scope for indexation would appear to be very great indeed.

It should come as no surprise to the reader to discover that the monetarist school adopts an attitude towards indexation which is diametrically opposed to that of the cost-push school. While most economists accept that indexation may go some way in enabling the economy to live with inflation, monetarists venture further than this, insisting that the indexation of money contracts will be extremely useful in *reducing* the rate of inflation. On the other hand the adherents to the cost-push view do not even accept that indexation makes inflation easier to live with. Instead they insist that the struggle for larger shares in the national income will be intensified rather than moderated by the widespread introduction of index-linked contracts. A brief outline of these two opposing views will be sketched out below.

The Monetarist Advocacy of Indexation[4]

Suppose the economy has inherited an actual and expected rate of inflation of 30 per cent per annum. According to the analysis of Chapter 4, workers will demand a 30 per cent increase in money wages over the coming year (abstracting from productivity growth) in order to defend the purchasing power of their wage packet. If, in such circumstances, workers could be persuaded that escalator clauses, incorporated into the wage contract, were a superior method of achieving the same end, monetarists argue that the actual rate of inflation would fall. By breaking the link between current wage bargains and anticipated changes in the price level, the rate of wage increase will respond much more sensitively to changing underlying conditions of supply and demand in the labour market. According to Jackman and Klappholz, '. . . by adjusting wages to *realized* rather than to *anticipated* inflation, indexation would make expectations of inflation irrelevant to wage settlements'.

In order to demonstrate this proposition Jackman and Klappholz, loyal to their monetarist convictions, assume that the authorities, dissatisfied with an excessively high rate of inflation, take steps to reduce the rate of monetary expansion. This would reduce the level of aggregate demand which would, in turn, temper the pace of wage and price increase: 'Once this starts to happen the indexation arrangements would again lead to a more rapid deceleration of the increase in wages, and hence in prices.'

Take the case of wages. The incorporation of escalator clauses into all money wage contracts would make wage bargaining a *real*

---

4. The analysis of this section relies heavily on a pamphlet by Jackman and Klappholz (1975) which goes into much greater detail on the arguments *pro* and *contra* indexation. However, the reader should note that the authors adopt a highly unsympathetic attitude towards the cost-push interpretation of inflation which they initially regard as 'implausible' but eventually condemn as logically 'groundless'.

phenomenon. Instead of negotiating in terms of money wages as before, the various participants in the wage bargain would effectively be negotiating in terms of real wages after the introduction of indexation. Trade union leaders should be persuaded that *this* is the best way of guaranteeing the living standards of their members. Moreover, since they hold that trade union leaders are reasonable men open to reasonable suggestion, Jackman and Klappholz regard union opposition as a relatively unlikely barrier to the introduction of general wage indexation. By accepting index-linked wage contracts, workers and employers are wiping the slate clean, ignoring past experience of inflation. They are setting their sights on the future, erasing from their minds all memory of wage negotiations which have gone before.

The 'hangover' of inflationary expectations generated by prior laxity in the conduct of monetary policy can thus be reduced to a minimum. The price level is released from the independent (though temporary) pressure on the side of wages, being determined exclusively by the supply of money. If, as they suggested, indexation is harnessed to a régime of strict monetary control, the effects of such a combined policy in reducing the rate of inflation with minimum unemployment could be dramatic. Wages will not rise unless prices rise; and prices will not rise unless the quantity of money is increased; hence indexation and monetary control together succeed in breaking the wage–price spiral where neither could succeed effectively when used in isolation.

Cost-Push Objections to Indexation

The attitude of most cost-push theorists towards indexation is predictably hostile. It is argued that if the root cause of inflation can be found in an irreconcilable struggle for higher shares in national income by competing socio-economic groups, a scheme which attempts to link *all* shares of the national cake to the general price level will simply exacerbate an already perilous situation. At its simplest the cost-push view states that, if workers are trying to wrest from capitalists a higher share of national income, and if capitalists nullify the workers' efforts by raising prices (aided, of course, by a pliable monetary authority), then the implementation of indexation which seeks to satisfy the demands for incompatible real shares *both* of workers *and* of capitalists will not only be ineffective, it will provide both groups with *carte blanche* for intensifying their socio-political power struggle. If demands for shares in national income are really 'non-negotiable' then the introduction of indexation will be worse than useless.

Consider, for example, the effects of a deterioration in the terms of trade produced by an increase in the price of imported oil. In the absence of significant productivity growth, real living standards must fall so as to prevent the balance of payments from running into deficit. If workers are subject to 'real-wage resistance' (see Chapter 7, page 106), they will respond to the higher price of goods and services resulting from the higher price of imported oil by lodging compensatory money wage claims. Indexation will not help, for it merely institutionalizes and legitimizes the phenomenon of real wage resistance.

The advocates of indexation respond to this objection by pointing out that money wage contracts could be linked, not to the *general* price level, which would include the higher prices of foreign goods and services and domestically produced goods which use imports as inputs into the productive process, but to a price index which specifically excludes the effects of variations in import prices. By linking money wage contracts to such an index, indexation will not impede the relative real wage adjustments which are occasionally required in order to maintain or restore balance of payments equilibrium. On the other hand, such a solution, even if it were accepted by trade unions (which is doubtful), would do little to reduce cost-push pressures of domestic origin, e.g. leapfrogging wage claims. Which brings us back to the general proposition that a necessary policy for the cure of a cost-push inflation is a policy of prices and incomes control.

Recommendations for Policy

When writing a book of this nature, the author must at some point lay his cards on the table and state his own personal view regarding the appropriate conduct of an anti-inflation programme. The final section of the last chapter is the ideal place for such self-indulgence.

Incomes Policy, Fiscal Policy and Monetary Policy

We have seen how the various cures for inflation which have been proposed over the last few years critically rest upon a particular theory of the causes of inflation. It can be argued that the current inflation being experienced in most of the industrialized countries of the West can, in large measure, be traced to cost-push factors which are independent of the forces of excess aggregate demand. By implication, therefore, the motive force for the recent inflation cannot be found in 'excessively lax' monetary and fiscal policies. Instead the motive force behind the recent inflation can be traced to a series of overlapping forces, all of which reinforce each other to put upward pressure upon the level of money wages. Three of these 'non-competitive' forces can be listed: (a) The desire of trade union negotiators to preserve the status of their members in relation to other groups of workers. Any threatened disruption of the 'accepted' status structure (leap-frogging) will be resisted by means of retaliatory wage claims. (b) The desire of negotiators to appropriate for their members a 'fair' share of any significant increase in their company's profits which, together with motive (a), could lead to an indefinite, and perhaps accelerating, wage–wage spiral. (c) Trade unions will try to resist any encroachment on the standard of living of their members caused by unfavourable external developments, such as a rise in the price of energy or of imported raw materials in terms of manufactured goods. This factor only occasionally comes into play, but when it does, inflation will be greatly accelerated as happened in 1974–5.

If this is an accurate thumb-nail account of the inflationary experience of the last decade – and many economists would dispute this – what are the policy implications of this view? One rather negative implication immediately stands out: if current inflation has virtually nothing to do with the past 'misconduct' of the monetary and fiscal authorities in the management of aggregate demand, then a policy of deliberate demand restriction will do little to curb inflationary pressure. A frequently heard riposte to this view is that, if demand restriction were pursued hard enough and for long enough, there would come a point where the unemployment rate was so high – say 20 per cent – that trade unions would start to moderate their demands for higher money wages. This *may* be true but it may also be felt to be a futile conjecture. If such an unemployment rate actually exists at which the 'market' cure for inflation begins to bite – and it is by no means obvious that it does exist – that unemployment rate is likely to be so high that the whole structure of the mixed economy might collapse before the monetarist cure starts to work. In other words, within the acceptable range of unemployment rates which most governments feel constrained to operate, the monetarist cure for inflation – a deflation of aggregate demand by monetary means alone – is unlikely to succeed in reducing the rate of increase of money wages.

But if the monetarist cure will not work, what will? The author would suggest that a policy of prices and incomes restraint must form the cornerstone of any anti-inflation policy. As was pointed out earlier, the precise form which such a policy would take would be a matter for negotiation among employers, the trade unions and the government. And it must be frankly admitted by anyone advocating another dose of such policies that their past track record cannot be described as glorious – in Britain, 'dismal' would be a more appropriate epithet. However, the important point to note is that the question of the determination, and hence the control, of money wages can no longer be analysed in narrowly economic terms: it has become very much a political problem.

If the principal onus of containing inflationary pressure is to be borne by an incomes policy, what role, if any, is to be played by fiscal and monetary policy? The answer to this question will strike many readers as quaintly old-fashioned. Fiscal policy should be the major instrument for controlling (but not fine-tuning) the level of aggregate domestic demand. Monetary policy should support fiscal policy in the sense of releasing unnecessary pressures upon the rate of interest which abnormally large budget deficits might produce. Obviously the objective – in the writer's view the desirable objective – of preserving 'orderly' financial markets and of ensuring the ready availability of credit at 'reasonable' interest rates to the business sector implies a high degree of complementarity between monetary and fiscal policies (see Chapter 6). However, the pursuit of rigid monetary targets, involving as it does erratic fluctuations in interest rates and the sporadic rationing of credit to the private sector, can do little to foster economic growth – quite the contrary – and will fail to achieve its stated objective, namely the elimination of inflation. Of course, if the government implements a successful incomes policy, the pursuit of inflexible monetary targets will cause less damage to the private sector than would have occurred under 'free' collective bargaining, but this is simply to observe that it is much easier to establish general financial stability with minimal disruption if inflationary pressures have been reduced by the instrument of incomes policy: a successful incomes policy makes the task of adhering to pre-announced monetary targets much easier.

But what about the knotty question of devaluation versus import controls as alternative solutions to the problem of payments imbalances? An elementary guide to the literature on inflation is hardly the place to expatiate on this subject, but in the author's opinion – an opinion *not* based on group loyalty – import controls are preferable to the large devaluation which would be required to achieve comparable 'real' effects upon output, employment and the balance of payments. In normal circumstances a managed floating of the exchange rate would probably suffice to maintain payments equilibrium in the market for internationally-traded goods. However, certain economies – and the British economy appears to be one of them – have travelled so far down the path of de-industrialization that only quite radical measures can arrest the process. Import controls are an important means of calling a halt to such industrial decline.

Trade Unions and Full Employment

If one accepts the view that there exists a rate of unemployment which corresponds to overall full employment in the labour market (Friedman calls this rate the natural unemployment rate), then the question which naturally arises is: Does the dominance of the trade union movement in the process of collective bargaining impede the attainment of full employment? In other words, does the existence of trade unions prevent the unemployment rate from falling to its full employment value?

This is a question on which the economist has virtually no evidence. Nevertheless many economists (the present author included) would support the opinion expressed by Hayek, who attributes a considerable proportion of the measured unemployment rate to the failure of *relative* wages (i.e. wages between occupations and industries) to adjust to changing conditions of supply and demand. The general acceptance of the principle of comparability with other groups of workers in wage negotiations renders the set of wage differentials highly unresponsive to varying supply/demand pressures in *individual* labour markets.

But if variations in wage differentials cannot be relied upon to reallocate labour under changing labour-market conditions, is there *any* mechanism which re-directs labour away from excess-supply sectors towards excess-demand sectors? The obvious answer would appear to be: relative unemployment rates. Labour will tend to move away from those sectors where unemployment is high towards sectors where it is low. Relative unemployment rates therefore replace (or at the very least reinforce) the role that variations in relative wages could play in allocating labour between different forms of employment. To the extent that the trade union movement is responsible for this inflexibility of relative wages, their existence will impart an upward bias on the overall measured unemployment rate. If one were to employ Friedman's terminology, one would say that the natural unemployment rate is higher in the presence of trade unions than it would be in their absence.

References

K.A. Chrystal, *Controversies in Britisn Macroeconomics*, Philip Allan, 1979.

F. Cripps and W.A.H. Godley, 'A formal analysis of the Cambridge Economic Policy Group Model', *Economica*, November 1976.

Phyllis Deane, in D. Heathfield (ed.), *Perspectives on Inflation*, Longman, 1979.

M. Friedman, *The Optimum Quantity of Money and Other Essays*, Macmillan, 1969.

M. Friedman, *Unemployment versus Inflation*, Institute of Economic Affairs, 1975.

M. Friedman, *The Times*, 13 September 1976.

M. Friedman, *Inflation and Unemployment*, Institute of Economic Affairs, 1977.

F.A. Hayek, *Full Employment at Any Price?*, Institute of Economic Affairs (Occasional Paper no. 45), 1975.

S.G.B. Henry, M.C. Sawyer and P. Smith, 'Models of inflation in the United Kingdom', *National Institute Economic Review*, August 1976.

J.R. Hicks, *The Crisis in Keynesian Economics*, Basil Blackwell, 1975(a).

J.R. Hicks, 'What is wrong with monetarism?', *Lloyds Bank Review*, October 1975(b).

A.G. Hines, 'Trade unions and wage inflation in the United Kingdom, 1893–1961', *Review of Economic Studies*, October 1964.

R. Jackman and K. Klappholz, *Taming the Tiger*, Institute of Economic Affairs (Hobart Paper no. 63), 1975.

Peter Jay, *The Times*, 15 April 1976.

R.F. Kahn, Evidence to the Committee on the Working of the Monetary System, Principal Memoranda and Evidence, 1959.

R.F. Kahn, *On Re-reading Keynes*, Proceedings of the British Academy, Vol. LX, 1975.

R.F. Kahn, 'Thoughts on the behaviour of wages and monetarism', *Lloyds Bank Review*, January 1976.

Nicholas Kaldor, 'The new monetarism', *Lloyds Bank Review*, July 1970.

Nicholas Kaldor, 'Inflation and recession in the world economy', *Economic Journal*, December 1976.

J.M. Keynes, *The General Theory of Employment, Interest and Money*, Macmillan, 1936.

J.M. Keynes, *How to Pay for the War*, Macmillan, 1940.

D. Laidler, in Lionel Robbins *et al.*, *Inflation: Causes, Consequences and Cures*, International Economic Association, 1974.

D. Laidler and M. Parkin, 'Inflation: a survey', *Economic Journal*, December 1975.

A. Leijonhufvud, *On Keynesian Economics and the Economics of Keynes*, Oxford University Press, 1968.

R.G. Lipsey, *An Introduction to Positive Economics*, Weidenfeld & Nicolson, 4th ed., 1975.

Edmond Malinvaud, *The Theory of Unemployment Reconsidered*, Basil Blackwell, 1977.

Donald Moggridge, ed., *The Collected Writings of John Maynard Keynes*, vol. XIV, Macmillan, for the Royal Economic Society, 1973.

Joan Robinson, *Economic Heresies*, Macmillan, 1971.

C.K. Rowley and A.T. Peacock, *Welfare Economics: A Liberal Restatement*, Martin Robertson, 1975.

J.A. Trevithick, 'Keynes, inflation and money illusion', *Economic Journal*, March 1975.

J.A. Trevithick, 'Money wage inflexibility and the Keynesian labour supply function', *Economic Journal*, June 1976.

J.A. Trevithick and C. Mulvey, *The Economics of Inflation*, Martin Robertson, 1975.

A.A. Walters, *Money in Boom and Slump*, Institute of Economic Affairs (Hobart Paper no. 44), 1971.

P. Wiles, 'Cost inflation and the state of economic theory', *Economic Journal*, June 1973.

Index